1988

The Graywolf Short Fiction Series

Feeding the Eagles

Short Stories by

Paulette Bates Alden

Graywolf Press

Saint Paul / 1988

The author is grateful to the editors of *The Antioch Review, The Greensboro Review, Kansas Quarterly, Mississippi Review* and *WARM Journal,* where some of these stories first appeared in slightly different form; and to the Bush Foundation and the Loft McKnight Awards for their generous support.

The Delmore Schwartz poem "Time's Dedication" is from *Selected Poems: Summer Knowledge.* Copyright © 1938 by New Directions Publishing Corporation. Used by permission.

ISBN 1-55597-111-3 (cloth)
ISBN 1-55597-116-4 (paper)
Library of Congress Catalog Card Number 88-81022
CIP data on last printed page

Publication of this book is made possible in part by grants from the Jerome Foundation, the General Mills Foundation, the National Endowment for the Arts, the Minnesota State Arts Board, and the many corporate, foundation and individual contributors to Graywolf Press. Graywolf Press is a member organization of United Arts, Saint Paul.

Published by Graywolf Press, Post Office Box 75006, Saint Paul, Minnesota 55175. All rights reserved.

9 8 7 6 5 4 3 2
FIRST PAPERBACK PRINTING, 1989

Contents

for Jeff

Feeding the Eagles

Blue Mountains

My husband is walking on the frozen river. I walk parallel to him, but on the brown ground of the bank. The water nearest the shore is not frozen, so I couldn't walk out onto the river here if I wanted to, which I don't. I grew up in South Carolina where the rivers never freeze. Earlier this winter, Ted and I walked out on Lake of the Isles near our house in Minneapolis. The ice was several feet deep, and green and white like quartz. Still, I couldn't wait to get back on the bank. Now, as Ted walks the river, it makes eerie sounds, like distant drum rolls under the ice. The sounds seem to originate from the far bank, a half mile away, but I can tell they are caused by his footsteps.

It was on this river, three years ago now, that I first understood that Ted and I would stay together. He had come home to visit his parents, and I came with him. We went sailing on this river. That summer day, the bluffs were so green they were almost black. There was something in the way Ted took my elbow to help me step out of the dinghy and climb onto the sailboat. He had very beautiful manners.

Huge ice slabs are piled along the shore where I walk. They lie heaped one upon the other as if drawn only to certain spots. Any block would be too heavy for a person to move. There must be currents in the river, under the ice, which propel them to just this place or that. Today in the sun they are dripping and milky white. It is fifty-five degrees, a record high for this day in February.

Ted has taken off his down jacket and knit cap. He is wearing the kind of clothes he always wears, the kind he has worn all his life—corduroy pants, an oxford-cloth shirt, a Shetland sweater—the clothes of his prep school days in St. Paul, even though he is thirty now. Whenever anything wears out, he replaces it with the identical thing. He knows exactly what he likes in clothes, and everything he wears seems right for him. His father and brothers wear the same kind of clothes. They all have blue blazers and grey flannel pants, and beautiful wool sport coats of soft natural colors. His mother wears the same kind of clothes, only for women. They shop at Gokey's in St. Paul, which never changes the style of clothes it sells, and which carries many items with ducks. Ducks on wastebaskets, throw pillows with ducks, duck ashtrays and cocktail glasses, ducks taking off on mailboxes and ducks lighting in the water on trays.

Ted and I married this summer, on the West Coast. We moved to Minnesota this fall, to live. Here, everything is familiar to Ted. Here, he has the land of his childhood, his family, this river which he loves. It makes me uneasy to see him walking on the frozen river. But of course he knows all about ice.

I spent my twenties saying I'd never marry. Then I married with hardly a thought. It only took ten minutes. We

4

were married in the courthouse of the neutral town in Washington State where we were living. Our next door neighbors were our witnesses. Later, describing it, Ted said it looked as if we were in traffic court. That was the way we wanted it; we didn't want much commotion.

I didn't know what to do about my name. There was never a moment when I had to decide. For the month or so before we moved, I used my regular name which was on my Washington driver's license and checks. Once we got here, I sent in a change of name card to Social Security, with my family name as my middle name, and Ted's name as my last name: Miriam Batson Swenson. The name was difficult to pronounce. I had trouble getting it out when I had to introduce myself. I was surprised how seriously people took such an awkward name, always taking care to say it all. I had assumed most people would drop my family name.

My mother, however, had no trouble with my name. She wrote me from South Carolina, addressing the envelope in her familiar hand with certainty: Mrs. Theodore F. Swenson, III.

Ted and I met in a writing class in San Francisco. He was staying with friends from college that spring, waiting to hear if he was accepted to law school. He had majored in English at Princeton; his honors thesis was on Scott Fitzgerald, another St. Paul boy. After college, he had tried a number of things—journalism, business school, writing. He was like the grasshopper in the story of the grasshopper and the ants. The grasshopper was not practical, but he was happy. Law school was Ted's latest idea on how to come to terms with the lesson of that story.

After college I had gotten a master's in English at

Berkeley. I had thought I would teach in high school. But
after six weeks of practice teaching, I realized I didn't want
to teach. I didn't want to have to have something to say
every day. I moved to San Francisco, and made my living in
hard ways, waitressing, temporary secretarial work, odd
part-time jobs that came and went. I was writing the history
of my family, my father gardening, my mother in her big
Buick. "You're the most sixties person I know," Ted said
when he first met me, before he got to know me.

That summer I went home with Ted when he visited his
folks, and we sailed on the blue river. He had been accepted
to law school and would begin in the fall. We hardly knew
each other. Still, I had no doubt that moving with him to
Washington was the right thing to do.

We went to a place that held nothing for us but each
other. Ted's law school was in a shopping center. We rented
an apartment like a motel room. It had wall-to-wall brown
carpets and white walls, and when we left three years later,
no one could tell we had ever lived there. I worked as a
waitress in a pseudo-Victorian restaurant with a view of
Puget Sound. I had to wear a long skirt and a high-collared
white blouse, as if I were in a play. In my off-hours I wrote.
Ted would come in from studying to find me at the
typewriter.

"What are you writing?"

"The history of my family."

"Again?"

Our main recreation was walking around the small lake
near our apartment complex. It was crowded with cottages
and suburban homes. I kept looking for something like our
cabin at Table Rock, where we spent the summers when I
was growing up. I wanted to show Ted. I could never adjust

my eye to the Douglas fir, the snowcapped Olympics to the west, the Cascades to the east, Mt. Rainier rising like an apparition. Landscape that meant nothing to me.

We told about our childhoods, his stories of cold, mine of heat. We went over and over the same things, reciting our personal myths, the history of our tribe of two.

"Maybe the thing is not to have kids," he would say. "Think of all the trouble, the responsibilities."

We talked about houses, children, cities, safe because they were still in the future, abstract. We thought aloud to each other, trying out possibilities: children, no children, a cabin in the woods, city life, the South, Minnesota, Seattle.

Sometimes he said to me, "Are you more like your mother or father?"

Sometimes I would say her, another time, him.

I would tell about the cabin, summers when I was a child, the big pale green luna moths hooking their hairy feet on the screen under the yellow outside light, the katydids, my parents rocking on the porch in the dark, the mountains the Cherokees called Ska-Ka-Na-Ga, the Great Blue Hills of God.

"If we had a child," Ted would say, "just think what he'd look like. My big head, your little one."

When we moved to Minnesota this fall, the Swensons had a big party to celebrate our marriage. They had a Mexican fellow roast a pig out back on the lawn overlooking the river. Ted had to help him carry the pig; it still had a head, tail, feet. The pig took all day to roast; grease leaked out of the oil drum onto the grass. The Swensons had a surprise wedding cake which Ted and I cut together in front of everyone. Several people took pictures, and everyone clapped.

The next day I called my parents in South Carolina. They seemed very far away over the wire, tiny. I didn't go into all the details. I could hear their wonder over the roasting of the pig, the big party. "We went to a pig roast once," my father shouted over the wire, but faintly. "It was in Hawaii." He meant on one of the trips he had won through his TV store. RCA sent the dealers to Japan, England, Hawaii. They got points for selling merchandise and won trips. But that was several years ago, before my father's business failed.

What had happened, no one knew. There were debts, the figures as fantastic and remote as the national debt. My parents had to sell their house. They sold, threw away, stored. By the time I came home that summer, a lot had disappeared.

My father closed his store. RCA came and took away all their merchandise. My father went to work as a salesman in the TV section of a department store in the mall. The TV section was on the second floor. It was a small, U-shaped space stacked with TVs. Eight or ten of them would be on at once, with no volume. Eight or ten wrestlers would shake their fists at the camera on Saturday afternoons, mouthing eight or ten voiceless threats.

For as long as I could remember—always!—my father had had his TV store on North Main Street. There was always a brown and white RCA dog in our lives, cocking his head in what I once thought was wonder, but which I now realize was puzzlement.

We drove out today, as we sometimes do on the weekends, to have Sunday dinner with Ted's parents. They live an hour out of the Twin Cities. Ted's younger brother Chip and his wife Nancy drove up from Rochester, where he is a resident at the Mayo Clinic. Nancy is expecting their first child in May. Ted's older brother Ben is also a doctor. Ted is the black sheep of the family; he can't stand the sight of blood.

Before dinner we sat in the living room which has beautiful handmade parquet floors, exposed beams in the high ceiling, and a wall of windows with a full view of the river. We didn't have a fire because of the temperature. We drank Campari and soda in wine glasses. Mine tasted bitter; I had never had such a drink. The Swensons discovered it in Italy this fall. Ted told a funny story about putting recycled oil in his car. The car is a '74 Mustang which uses two quarts of oil a week. When he said "Fill it to the rim with Vim," explaining what he says at the service station, everyone laughed. He is the funniest member of the family. The way he says things makes people laugh.

Nancy and I helped Amelia, Ted's mother, get the dinner on the table. The cabinets are full of dishes: Mexican pottery, Italian china, English ironstone. I was afraid I would break something. When I got down the Italian plates, white with red bands, I felt something would become unbalanced and crash to the floor.

At the dinner table there was a great deal of conversation. Ted's mother and father sit at either end of the table. There is always a lot of talk here. Dr. and Mrs. Swenson—John and Amelia—have a great deal to say; they sometimes tell the same story at the same time, interrupting or correcting each other. They're in the prime of their lives, and their energy often makes Ted and me tired. We'll go home this evening exhausted.

Across the table from me, Ted talked a great deal. So much talk makes him talk more. He wakes up talking, goes to sleep talking. He talks for the pleasure of his own voice, the way dogs bark and birds sing.

"I don't think Nancy has any special maternal feelings," Chip, next to me, told me. Around us everyone was talking the Walker, the Guthrie, Robert Motherwell at Landmark Center. "It's just that we decided now was the time to go ahead. We figured we wanted a child someday, but there was never a moment when we were ready."

He tells me this because I'll be thirty-four this spring.

"Now I have to admit," he says, grinning like a boy, not like a doctor who cuts into people's chests, "I'm thrilled about it."

We eat quail and wild rice off the Italian plates. Dr. Swenson serves the plates from the head of the table, and thinks, perhaps, that because all three women present are thin that they don't eat much. I usually have to get something at home after we have dinner here.

We went to South Carolina this past Thanksgiving, after we got settled. Ted's mother paid for our airline tickets. She wanted to make sure my parents didn't feel left out.

My mother had put on weight. When I hugged her, she felt round and hard in her girdle. All her life she has gained and lost, gained and lost. Her shoulders were very small.

My father got tears in his blue eyes when he shook Ted's hand. The TV was on in the den when we arrived and they didn't turn it off, but they did turn it down. There was always a TV on when I was growing up.

My father wanted to know about our TV. It is the small black-and-white one he had given me in college. He couldn't understand why we don't have a color one. It didn't occur to him that we don't watch much TV. He was interested to know about the Swensons' TV. They have a small color one in the library, which they turn on rarely, to watch simulcasts of symphonies, or ETV. My parents like Rockford, they like the news and weather, the Today program, gospel singing, Johnny Carson.

We show my parents the pictures taken at the pig roast. Ted and me cutting the cake. The Mexican fellow with the pig. The Swensons' handsome friends with bright picnic trays on their laps. My mother holds the picture of Amelia Swenson sitting in the grass in her peasant skirt from Guatemala for an extra moment. "I didn't realize your mother was so young!" she says to Ted. She means this as a compliment, but the expression on her face is one of bewilderment.

We spend the time watching TV and eating. My mother fixes the food I grew up on and love, but don't fix myself: field peas cooked with fat back and red pepper; a roast steamed to pieces in its own juices in the pressure cooker; fried chicken, cream gravy, okra, cornbread. I eat leftovers every night, holding a plate in my lap in the La-Z-Boy rocker in the den while we watch the ten o'clock news.

On Sunday morning my father cooks us a big country ham breakfast. He is happy in the kitchen in his barbecue apron, proud of the country ham. He saws off extra slices and wraps them in Saran Wrap and puts them in a plastic bag for me to take back in our suitcase. He knows I cannot get country ham in Minnesota. He makes redeye gravy by pouring hot coffee in the pan drippings, sizzling it all down to half a cup. The kitchen is steamy with the smell of it. Poured in a bowl, the grease rises to the top and the red eye stares up from the bottom. We have scrambled eggs and yellow grits the way we always do, on Red Vista dishes. My mother fixes homemade biscuits the way she does, thin and barely brown.

On Monday before we leave my mother and I go shopping. When I was growing up, she took me to expensive women's stores where thin ladies in good white slips padded in their stocking feet on the thick carpets. There was actually a time in my life when I wore tailored suits, high heels, hose attached to garter belts, hats, and white gloves. Though I no longer own any white gloves, sometimes, stirring around in my underwear drawer, I can almost feel them there, mismatched and smudged with my adolescent makeup.

Now when I come home, "having nothing to wear," as my mother puts it, is a problem. My clothes come from stores with names like Incaland and Global Village. In an outlet store of a local textile mill, my mother holds up double-knit suits and polyester blouses to me hopefully. But I cannot find anything I would ever wear, and so we go home empty-handed. My mother shakes her head. She cannot understand why I prefer natural fabrics, one hundred percent cottons, rayons, linens, things that look wrinkled on the racks.

When it came time for me to go to college, my mother drove me around to look at schools in South Carolina and North Carolina. She had spent the years of my childhood waiting in the front seat of her blue Buick, reading *House Beautiful* or *Reader's Digest* while I had this lesson or that.

I went to college a hundred miles from home. I didn't consider graduate school until a professor who had taken an interest in me encouraged me. When he mentioned Berkeley, I had never heard of it. Still, once I understood, I had no doubt that I should go. It was as if something were propelling me, a current which moved me in that direction, though it took me, perhaps, farther than I ever intended to go.

Now it is winter, and Ted walks the frozen river. I stand on the bank. Lately, on these bright mornings, just as I am waking, I believe that I am at the cabin. I am a child again, it is summer, I am at the cabin with my parents, it is the hot Southern sun that wakes me. But I am in Minnesota, lying next to my husband, and it is winter. Stretching out around us in every direction are the flat Midwestern plains, and it comes to me that I will not live my life as I have always imagined I would—without even thinking of it—in South Carolina. I will not open my eyes in the morning and close them at night to the shape of blue mountains. *And not to have a Southern child!*

Ted is far down the river now, the only figure on the broad white expanse. My eye flies to him—a funny, happy man! I remember how when we first came here, he went to his old room and got exactly what he needed. Everything was just as he had left it. Nothing had been taken away, or lost.

Now that I stand very still, I am aware of tiny sounds emanating from the ice near the shore. Tiny tappings, inquisitive, like insects hitting glass, the sounds of fragmentation, separation. The ice must be expanding and contracting imperceptibly, shifting ever so slightly in preparation for the spring thaw. One would not even notice unless standing very still, quiet and alone. In a few weeks it will be spring.

Legacies

Miriam stands by with the towel while her grandmother bends over and washes her hair at the kitchen sink. The old woman has taken off her blouse, and has on an odd contraption which must be a brassiere, though it has no cups that Miriam can see, and is down around her waist, where her breasts have come to rest. Miriam helps her rinse her head by pouring boilers of warm water through her hair, catching the suds at her grandmother's neck with the edge of her finger. She helps her grandmother, whose name is Maud, wrap her head in a turban of terrycloth. They move in slow motion, which gives each action a sense of importance, the feeling of ritual. Maud turns now and commences her slow wide-gaited walk to the bedroom. Miriam follows close behind, and stands like a lady-in-waiting while her grandmother takes her seat on the dresser stool.

Now Miriam will roll her grandmother's hair, though she is squeamish about scalps. She does not like to see through the wet cords of grey hair to the whiteness beneath. It causes a pang of emotion in her when she must put the sharp teeth of the comb against her grandmother's exposed and vulnerable head. Her grandmother, however, is not so delicate. "Don't worry about hurting me," she says, "I'm tough headed," and she roughs up her hair with fingers stiff and bent with arthritis, which are not so much like fingers as tools. Miriam takes seriously the business of combing out the hair, which she expects to be tangled and recalcitrant, but which gives way before her comb with ease.

And here are the curlers, a stationary box full of odds and ends, some of which Miriam recognizes as her old ones from high school. Here are the pink ones with plastic snap-on tops, and others with long toothpicks to push through to hold them. Meanest looking of all are the wire ones with brushes inside, and the sharp bobby pins with their protective tips worn off. Her grandmother takes the comb from Miriam and shows her where the part should be, and tells how Frances, the preacher's wife, usually rolls it. She settles down contentedly, holding the box in her lap, handing curlers to Miriam, who would prefer to pick them out herself, before she is ready.

Though her grandmother talks constantly now, unwilling to lose a moment of their time together in silence, Miriam says hardly a word, nor is she particularly listening. All her attention is absorbed in the difficulty of coiling the unruly hair, which is drying too fast, around the curlers. She is afraid of the moment when she must push the pin in, though her grandmother doesn't seem to mind at all. There is an air conditioner, but they do not turn it on because of Maud's arthritis, and the heat of the South Carolina afternoon, along with her grandmother's voice and the feel of the drying hair in her hands, have put Miriam into a trance, a state close to sleep in which she feels far away, or underwater.

It is always like this. For all the years of her life that Miriam has been old enough to be always going away, and always returning, they have repeated the rhythm of this summer day, though it may take place in the fall or winter or spring. It is always her grandmother and it is always Miriam, the mimosa outside the window buds and blooms and disappears to bud and bloom all pink and green again. There is always the apartment, there is always heat and sleep, and her grandmother's voice winding on and on while Miriam attends.

Though it has seemed over the years that there was a constancy here as permanent as that which always is, Miriam finds that while she was away this last time some things have changed. Though all appears the same, though everything is in place, and her grandmother sits as always under Miriam's hands, something is different. For this time her grandmother asks again and again the same question and Miriam answers again and again the same answer, and this is something different. And now there is the bathroom door, which before Miriam has taken for granted as just a door. But this time it is an offender. It was this door which Maud reached out for like a friend when she started to fall, but which opened and carried her with it, depositing the old woman in a heap on the floor. They had been expecting this fall forever, until the expectation became a part of the constancy, so that they were not prepared for the actual event, the moment of change when the door swung open and Maud fell down. It was one of Edith's days, and she got Maud into bed, and called Miriam's mother across town. When Mrs. Batson arrived, Maud pronounced the worst: she had finally broken her back. But when Miriam's mother started to take off her old lady black shoes, Maud sat straight up in bed, bent over, and undid them herself.

By the time Miriam came home in the summer, the fall was old news. Since there had been no broken bones, Miriam wanted to believe that things could go on the way they always had, her grandmother and the apartment, the mimosa and heat and sleep. But how strange it was the way her grandmother couldn't remember from one moment to the next. How slippery, elusive, the present had become, though the past was perfectly intact. But in the present there were necessities, medicine to take, the stove to turn off. And Maud couldn't remember this and she couldn't remember that. And knew that she couldn't remember. So while it was true that nothing had been broken, that was not the same as saying that everything was still whole.

Miriam has finished with the hair, except for the straight ends at the back of her grandmother's neck, too short even for pin curls. Her grandmother asks for a net, and Miriam certainly agrees, for from her vantage point above she sees that something else is needed to hold the precarious construction of curlers in place. Luckily her grandmother remembers exactly where she keeps a net, and in almost no time at all—for normally things take forever here—Miriam stretches the thin grey web over her grandmother's head, twists it in back, and secures the whole thing with a bobby pin.

"Are you tired?" Miriam asks. Maud has swung her legs around with her hands, as if they are paralyzed, and faces Miriam, who has sat down on the bed, for it is she herself who is tired. There is the summer heat, the small apartment, and her grandmother's need to talk, her need, and the repetition of questions which Miriam must answer again and again and again. Always in the afternoons her grandmother takes a nap, and Miriam will fall asleep on the extra bed in the living room, and sleep with her mouth open, waking with the sense that she has been deeply unconscious. Now she wants nothing more than to go into the living room and lie down by herself, away from her grandmother. What she desires is oblivion. So perhaps her grandmother will rest now, and leave Miriam be.

"I can rest when you go," her grandmother says. "When did you say your mother was coming for you?"

For the fourth time Miriam tells her. It will be late afternoon before her mother can pick her up. She is at the beauty parlor getting a new permanent. So why not rest now?

But her grandmother is already thinking of something else. It seems to Miriam that her grandmother, as she gets older, is not fading but rather becoming more concentrated. She makes Miriam, at twenty-eight, feel somehow diluted and vague, still unformed. Now her grandmother is hobbling back into the living room, catching on things with each step like a drunk person—the image makes Miriam smile, for to her grandmother there is no greater sin than drink. How strictly, with what a severe and self-righteous religiosity, Maud raised Miriam's mother—no dancing, no playing cards, no drinking! Of course Miriam's mother has turned out to enjoy all these activities, though hardly as devil's work, ruination. The bridge playing, Exchange Club dances, and neighborhood cocktail parties that constitute her parents' social life seem so modest and harmless to Miriam she can't help but resent the double life her mother has to lead where Maud is concerned.

Her grandmother sits down heavily on the sofa. Miriam sits beside her, and they face not each other, but the opposite wall of the living room.

"When did you say you're going back?"

"Tomorrow," Miriam says. Her time at home is almost over. They have reached that part of the visit when she is with her grandmother for the "last time." For so many years when it was time to say goodbye, Miriam would think: this will be the last time I will see her. There have been so many emotional partings, too many. Her grandmother is eighty-five now, and Miriam can no longer believe that she will really die. Instead, her grandmother seems to be caught in some perpetual motion that will go on and on. It is no longer her death that weights Miriam's heart but her life—that it go on and on, wearing down their emotions, numbing their love, the fear that she will become a problem, a Problem, and little more.

"Do you have to go back so soon," her grandmother says. "Seems like I haven't seen much of you this time."

This part of the conversation makes Miriam uncomfortable, guilty, for she can hardly wait for the moment tomorrow when the little Eastern plane will lift her up, out, and away from her hometown. There will be the short hop to Atlanta, and then a 727 will take her all the way across the country, where she can float free, away from the entanglements of the South, her family, her grandmother, and even herself to a large extent. Odd how as soon as she leaves, she begins thinking of when she can return.

"You like it way out there?" her grandmother asks, as she always does. "Way out there wherever it is you live?"

Miriam feels her ears burning a little. This is one of her grandmother's favorite subjects, next to her "baby" and

God. She cannot understand why Miriam wants to live three thousand miles away from them all. "I like it fine, Grandmother," she says, in what sounds even to her like a lame voice. Actually, she could care less about San Francisco, or the whole West Coast for that matter. On the other hand, the problems out there are not her problems, are not the problems here, and she doesn't have to claim them.

"I've been thinking," her grandmother says. "Your mother told me you don't have much in the way of furniture—out there—wherever it is you live. I was thinking maybe you'd like to have my things when I have to move out of here."

Miriam looks around her in dismay. She can just imagine her mother putting a bid in for Miriam to get the furniture. Given the life she has led, moving around, never marrying, her mother assumes she has cut herself off from material possessions. But what can she be thinking? In any other setting her grandmother's things would be ludicrous. Really—who can imagine such ugly stuff, though before, Miriam has taken it for granted, hardly noticed it. But she recoils from the idea of it someday being hers—she would never have it—the awkward drop-leaf table, completely without grace; the yellow satin rocker—downright awful; the enormously heavy green couch covered with a throw from Penney's; those baroque single beds, looking like something out of a German nightmare.

And besides, the furniture would always smell to Miriam like her grandmother, like her grandmother's apartment, and there's no getting around it, the place smells like shit. Miriam's mother calls her grandmother's colostomy "her baby," and in truth she is always cradling it there on her side, nursing it, wiping it, and worst of all talking about it all the time—doting on it almost! At the time of the operation thirty years ago, she said she didn't want the rerouting operation which would put things back in their natural place; thought she was going to die anyway, and was too sick to care. But of course she lived, and came home from the hospital with her "baby" to devote her attention to from then on.

For as long as Miriam can remember, her grandmother's place has always been full of wide-mouthed quart jars, and plastic bags which her grandmother washes and reuses. The bags are everywhere, hanging from a line over the bathtub, airing out in the bedroom window, and there are even some in the icebox, stored in an old Russell Stover chocolate box. Sometimes when Miriam watches her grandmother eat she can't help thinking where all that food will end up. She has often sat like a captive audience, held by a morbid fascination, while her grandmother tells how she has had to "work it out," her crooked fingers perched on that side of her, or how she is taking medicine to "check it." She is always "working it out" or "checking it."

"Couldn't you use some of my things?"

"Well, maybe someday," Miriam hedges. "But I don't have any way to take anything back with me now. Anyway—you'll be using things yourself for awhile yet. Don't be giving everything away before you have to."

Her mother has told her not to mention the business of a nursing home, though clearly it is on her grandmother's mind, as well as her own. Her mother has been making arrangements for the time when Maud can no longer live on her own. Still—they hope that Maud will just be able to die in her own place. She will hardly discuss the nursing home. But since the fall, she has begun to give things away, and usually not to the right people, according to Miriam's mother.

"When you gonna come back this way for good?" Her grandmother doesn't look at her. They talk into the air. Miriam sees with peripheral vision her grandmother's profile, which reminds her of a cameo. She has her hands folded in her lap.

"I don't know, Grandmother."

"I was thinking of giving Elmo this coffee table." She indicates the weird item in front of them. It has been there since time immemorial, and Miriam has never really looked at it before. It is too high for a coffee table, but she cannot guess what else it might be. It has curved French provincial legs painted white, which look as if they have rickets, and its top is scalloped deeply all around. She cannot imagine that her uncle Elmo, an old man now himself, a thousand miles away in Texas would give a hoot about the table, not to mention the problem of getting it to him. Concerning what to do about their mother, he writes to Miriam's mother to "do whatever she thinks best," as if that were any help. Yet, of course, he has always been Maud's "favorite."

"I've been thinking. If I do have to move out of here, I could just move in with your mother. They've got that downstairs bedroom, and I could stay out of their way. I could give them the money I'd just be pouring down the drain to strangers in a nursing home."

Her grandmother is full of surprises. Miriam has to resist the impulse to turn to her and say, "Why, Grandmother, you must be crazy!" She continues to sit in her somnolent state on the couch, but she cannot help snorting through her nose, this idea of her grandmother moving in with her parents strikes her as so preposterous, impossible, absurd, unbelievable! They've joked about it for years, Miriam and her mother, the way people do about their worst fears. Her mother always says, "The day she moves in here is the day I move to Columbia"—their shorthand for the state mental hospital. For this idea has surfaced and been routinely squashed, for years. But here it comes again like crab grass—you can't get to the root of the thing. Miriam can just see her father coming home after a hard day's work, and wanting to "take a drink," and there's Grandma, stinking up the place with her baby, into everybody's business with a vengeance, it's Billy Graham this and Oral Roberts that. Not that Miriam's mother entertains the slightest idea of being a martyr. She is too schooled in self-defense for that. But Miriam finds it annoying how her grandmother keeps on with what the whole world can see is out of the question. It makes what is already hard, harder.

"Oh, Grandmother. Don't go worrying about that now. You're getting along all right here by yourself for awhile."

"I don't see why it wouldn't work out—but your mother won't hear a word of it."

"Well, Grandmother—I just don't think it would work out. I mean—Mama already has to take care of Daddy, he's getting old and works so hard. Besides, they don't really have room for you."

"Well, all I know is they could use the money, better than it going to strangers."

This is not really the issue of course. What money she has left is a pittance, her Social Security and Veteran's not even enough to cover the nursing home care. When Miriam's mother tried to talk to her about the money, she said that she had tithed all her life, and was sure the Lord would take care of her now. But as her mother told Miriam, so far He hadn't stepped forward with any checks, and so it looked as if they'd have to lean on the everlasting arms of the government.

"I could stay in my room, and not get in their way. I'd have Edith come two days there just like she does here, and that would help your mother out." Her grandmother's voice is growing in intensity. Her hands have come to life, flying around in the air.

"But in a nursing home you'd always have someone to look after you, company. They'd fix your diet there. Mama can't stay home all day and look after you. Why you'd be lonely at Mama's."

"I'm used to being alone. I'm alone all the time."

"But you know about two women trying to rule the same roost. I'm not so sure you and Mama could get along. Even family who love each other sometimes can't live together."

"Well, I can't even imagine your mother not taking me in in my old age! That's what families are for! It's only right. I'd be less trouble for her than I am now, what with calling and bringing the groceries way over here every week. I'm getting so old and forgetful. I don't know how much longer I can keep on here myself."

Her grandmother is growing more excited, argumentative, stubborn. She speaks in what for her is a loud voice. And Miriam finds herself locked into the same kind of hardheadedness; she would like to force her grandmother once and for all to give up this nonsense (which makes too much sense), to let it go, because it will never be. It is intolerable the way her grandmother won't accept what is, won't face up to the facts, but no, she just keeps on and on no matter what price other people will have to pay. Miriam's mother is sixty-five! Will she always have this old woman on her back? But of course her mother would never argue with Maud like this. She is just waiting for what will be, will be. In the meantime, maybe Maud will die, and it won't come to a nursing home. Miriam knows that she should stop, but she feels the need for the last word, and she knows just what she wants that word to be: nursing home. Ironic, really, for she is sickened by the thought of her grandmother having to go to a nursing home.

"Grandmother, maybe you should at least consider a nursing home. Mother and I went to see one called Oakview last week, and it really was nice. Won't you at least go and look at it?"

They had thought Miriam should see Oakview while she was home. It was a long, low red-brick complex just outside the city limits, the sort of building you never notice until you have to. When they went in, they saw two of the old ones, sitting in chairs there in the foyer, a small table between them, though they seemed oblivious to each other's presence. The man had a big round stomach like a beach ball which he seemed to be holding in his lap, one good eye and one gone haywire; he was talking to himself in a high babble. He reminded Miriam of a cartoon figure, abstracted and exaggerated. She found that she was hugging herself, and had to make a conscious effort to loosen her arms from around herself.

A social worker, a woman about Miriam's age, showed them around, and everything was clean and cheerful in an institutional way. There were so many ancient ones. Taken alone any one of them would have been no worse—no more human—than her grandmother, but taken all together, their infirmities and grotesqueries added up, accumulated, until it was impossible to see the people themselves. Miriam noticed that her mother fell silent, and so Miriam carried on in a polite social role, asking a lot of questions in an abstract way, which she realized later had nothing to do with her grandmother. She detached herself from it all, as if she were a professional, a social worker herself, and not a grand-daughter. When she and her mother rode home afterwards, they had little to say. Miriam felt that underneath a facade of normalcy they were both in shock. For her part, she couldn't believe that any of it had anything to do with her grandmother, for it was all so impersonal, indifferent, and their old woman was becoming moment by moment all the more personal, demanding. Self.

Her grandmother dismisses the subject of the nursing home with a flick of her hand, dismissing with it Miriam's hope of making everything all right. "I could just move into that downstairs bedroom, and help your folks out. I know I wouldn't be a bother."

"But at the nursing home.... "

"As long as I can do for myself.... "

"That's right but.... "

"But when the time comes, I don't see why.... "

"Grandmother—it won't work."

"I wouldn't be any trouble, just stay.... "

"Grandmother! Please!"

Her grandmother starts at Miriam's sharp voice. "What is it?" she says, and for the first time since they have sat down she looks right at Miriam, her old eyes searching.

"Grandmother—it's just that I'm tired. I feel so sleepy,

just like I've been drugged. Aren't you tired? You must be! Why don't we just rest a little? Then we'll have our snack? All right?"

"The way I'm hurting so bad all over, I guess I better lie down a little while."

She gets up wearily, but Miriam continues to sit on the couch, immobilized. She can hardly bear the familiar figure of her grandmother moving so slowly, like a dream figure, towards the bedroom. But even as she feels pity she resents it, for her grandmother is like a vacuum that sucks up all one's sympathy and asks for more. She is like some primeval form of life concerned only with its own survival, ready to devour everything if only it can live.

Miriam puts her head back on the couch, exhausted, and immediately falls into a waking sleep. She sees her mother and herself on a two-man life raft, and yet there is the old woman, her grandmother, clinging to the side, trying to climb on board, to save herself even if it means capsizing them. Miriam and her mother are the survivors, they have the right to live! But the old lady will pull them all under. Miriam tries to pry her hands off, to make her let go. If only her grandmother will just give up, float off, accept the inevitable. It doesn't have to be so hard as she is making it! But she won't let go, she clings with an amazingly tenacious grip! Then Miriam in her fury begins to kick at her grandmother's hands, she kicks and kicks and kicks. . . .

The violence of the fantasy shakes Miriam out of her trance. Her eyes, lost at sea, search for something to anchor her, and they fix upon her grandmother's hanging vine at the window. This plant with its shiny green leaves is so innocent and harmless looking that Miriam feels stunned. She has a plant just like it, grown from a cutting she took back to

San Francisco with her one year, carried in her lap on the plane.

She gets up and goes quietly into the bedroom to see if her grandmother is all right. If only she would find her dead, gone off peacefully in her sleep. But she is only sleeping, her mouth open, her hook nose emitting the belabored sound of breath. Miriam bends closer, to see what the eye will see: the blackheads of her nose, the white hairs sprouting from her chin, the worn silk of skin. And with her hair bound in curlers her face is all the more exposed. Miriam realizes she hardly knows what her grandmother looks like she is so used to her. The sight of her naked face now is as awesome to Miriam as some ancient artifact she might see in a museum, and as familiar as a glass of milk. She sees what she will see one day: her grandmother dead. The moment *will* come when they will be free of the pain, guilt, suffering, and loneliness of her grandmother's old age. The moment will come, and take them all by surprise, even though they are ready for it, prepared, eager even. She feels the shock of it, and it is not as she would have thought—relief, release—for what is this sudden pain that bursts in her throat, blocking her breath, and what is this ripping apart, this loneliness, this loss? She would have thought that where her grandmother was concerned, her emotions would be worn down to numbness. But what a wealth of them she has left, more than she needs. She turns away, blinded.

It is late afternoon when Miriam hears her mother's car on the cement driveway outside. And all at once her mother is there, dressed in one of her summer dresses, a bright gay thing all pink and green. She has a new permanent and her golden hair (though surely it has been grey for years) is sculpted into a kind of bravado against her own old age. At the sight of her, Miriam's eyes fill again, mysteriously.

"How have y'all been getting along?" her mother asks her, in her ironic voice, for she knows exactly what it has been like.

Before Miriam can speak, her grandmother appears in the doorway, afraid of missing something.

"I see you got your hair rolled."

Maud feels it all over with her hands. "Wonder if it's dry yet. Sure don't want to have to sleep on these things tonight."

"Y'all must be burning up," her mother says. She goes over and turns on the air conditioner, and Miriam feels a sudden blast of cold air, which she remembers vaguely from another world.

Her mother is looking through the mail on the coffee table, passing over a letter from Uncle Elmo. She writes a check for Maud's water bill, seals the envelope, and puts it in her purse to mail.

"Don't you'all want some ice cream?" the old lady asks.

"We better get on home," Miriam's mother says, predictably. She doesn't like to stay long enough at Maud's to get stuck. She goes in the kitchen, looks through the icebox, and throws out an empty egg carton. "You and Edith been through here to throw anything out lately?"

"You know," Maud says from the living room. "I've noticed some red spots around my opening here." She pats her baby. "Seems like it might be all swollen and red somehow, like something's wrong."

"When did you first notice it?" Miriam's mother says. She comes back into the living room and stands before them. Miriam can almost feel along the inside of her arms her mother's body, her hips round and hard from her girdle, her shoulders surprisingly small—the way she will feel tomorrow when Miriam hugs her goodbye. She feels almost that she cannot leave them, that leaving is too hard, too painful. It is a painful gift that her mother has given her, the freedom to go, to be. She feels almost as if she cannot bear it, will not be able to go through with it.

Her grandmother taps her fingers against her forehead. "Now when was it? Been a day or two I believe. I think I wrote it in my daily diary. Now where did I put it?" And she starts to get up.

"Never mind," Miriam's mother says, stopping her. "I better have a look."

Maud pulls down the elastic of her pants over her big white stomach. Miriam's mother bends over to see. Watching her mother, Miriam thinks how mere love is a luxury. There is a feeling beyond love, which is more than love, which is what life requires.

"It doesn't look like anything to me," her mother says. "It's always been like that."

"I guess I just never noticed before."

"Well, pull your pants up. We'll take your hair down before we leave."

They move into the bedroom, where her grandmother sits again on the dresser stool. With quick sure hands her mother takes out the curlers. "Remember these," she says to Miriam.

"My hair used to be long enough to sit on," her grandmother tells Miriam, looking for her in the mirror until she finds her on the bed. "It would take so long to wash and comb out, I don't know why I even wanted such long hair. I'd wear it on top of my head in a bun."

"She had it cut off in a long pigtail," Miriam's mother says. She is trying to tease Maud's hair with a comb, for there is not much curl; the hair is not completely dry. "Then she wore that as a hairpiece for years."

With a memory that amazes Miriam, her grandmother says, "Why I bet that's still in my bottom dresser drawer. I believe that's where I put it when I moved from the big house."

Miriam opens the bottom dresser drawer. Here are her grandmother's underthings, which have always seemed to Miriam more intimate and certainly more complex than mere pants and bras. The smell of rose petals emanates. She sinks her hands down into the cool white stacks of nylon, and comes up with a plastic bag, inside of which she sees something that looks like a long, thin animal. She finds herself strangely excited. It is very brown—she can't remember when her grandmother's hair wasn't grey, though there is a photograph of her as a big buxom woman with dark hair, twice her present size, a complete stranger, holding the hand of another stranger, Miriam's mother as a long-legged blonde child with bangs. Her mother takes the hair from the bag, and drapes it across her hand. She shows it to Maud, who touches it lightly. They all stare at it. Then her mother and grandmother turn and look at the top of Miriam's head.

Miriam feels herself recoil. "Oh no," she says, laughing a little, nervously. She's not so sure she likes the hair. A shiver passes through her.

"Try it," her mother says. She hands it over to Miriam.

It is done up with some kind of binding at the top, and is still fixed in a loose pigtail, though fine hair is flying from it in a kind of delicate explosion. It is glossy, as if freshly washed.

"I never expected to see that again," her grandmother says in wonder.

In spite of herself, Miriam turns her head over, and her mother brushes her straight fine hair into something resembling a little knot on top and secures it with a rubber band. "Sit here," her grandmother says, giving up her place on the dresser bench. Miriam is too tall for her mother, and so she sits, and her mother wraps the hair piece around her top knot, to make a kind of coil. The color is remarkably near Miriam's own. Her mother is sticking pins in all around to hold it. Miriam trembles a little. When it is relatively secure, they all lean over to see Miriam in the mirror. And there they are, the grey, the brown, the golden, framed in the big oval mirror, studying the already falling apart crown which Miriam's mother has constructed for Miriam out of her grandmother's hair. Then Miriam is having to catch the hairpiece which is sliding off her head and down her back as if alive, pulling her own hair painfully with it. Pins shoot every-which-way.

"It's perfect for you!" her mother exclaims, with the optimism of someone who always thinks last year's styles will come back in again.

"Oh, Mother. I'd never wear it."

"Well you just take it on," her grandmother says. "I want you to have it. It'll just get lost or stolen around here."

"I don't know, Grandmother," Miriam says. She tries to hand it back.

"You've got to take it," her mother says. "What else are we to do with it?" And she pushes it back firmly into Miriam's hands.

And there it is. It is strange stuff, this old young hair. But her mother is right. What in the world will become of her grandmother's hair if Miriam doesn't take it? It strikes her as some unwanted pet for which she must now be responsible. Where will she keep it? She'll have it forever, it will always be there in her bottom drawer. She looks at her grandmother and mother, suspecting a conspiracy, but they have forgotten her or so it seems. She looks down at the hair. She strokes it a little, trying to make friends.

In a Piney Wood

If it had not been almost dark, and if they had not driven five hundred miles that day, and if she had thought they could find any other place at all, she would have asked him to go on, for there was something so deserted and ugly about the state park—but there was no choice.

The young man had suggested they just pull off on a side road somewhere and spend the night. That way they wouldn't waste any money. But she had told him she wouldn't sleep at all where any stranger might come upon them in the night, though she knew, of course, that she was being ridiculous.

She had been reading the campbook off and on for an hour to find a campground in this area of Tennessee. She needed a good night's rest. They had been traveling across the country hard and fast for several days and it didn't go well with her. When she discovered this particular state park in the book, she had felt an overwhelming sense of relief. It was twenty miles out of their way, but at least they would be safe, and even have toilet and shower facilities.

When she saw the place she didn't know what she had been expecting. Naturally it was just like the country they had been traveling through all afternoon—dense with tall skinny pines—the ugliest trees she had ever seen—and nothing but red dirt and flat land. She told him she would be glad when they got out of Tennessee—who could live in such a place? He reminded her that she was the one who had wanted to stop for the night. He said he could drive all night.

She objected. He was bound to be tired, traveling the way they were. And even if he wasn't, she was. She was dog tired. Besides, why not make the trip pleasurable? They didn't have to be back to California for a week.

That was true, he said, but was she forgetting they had to find a place to live? September was the hardest time of all for cheap student housing. They'd be lucky to get anything.

He pulled the VW bus over in front of the entrance booth. She got the kitty, which they kept in a Kodak film box, from the glove compartment. When she stepped down from the bus every bone in her body ached, and the small of her back felt as if it had been in traction. A middle-aged woman was in the booth, and she wouldn't look directly into the face of the young woman. The young woman thought this was because the woman suspected that she and the young man were not married, which was true, and that the woman with her stupid, provincial Tennessee ways disapproved. The woman's closed manner made her feel ashamed, and therefore angry, but she tried to be especially nice and friendly. She smiled, but the woman made no response. The young woman thought for an instant of her own parents, and her face felt hot as if with fever.

The camp site cost two dollars. Were they only staying

one night? Yes, just passing through. Around her it was steadily growing darker. The young woman was sure that no one would come to this park if he could help it. She couldn't imagine why the state would build a park in such a godforsaken place, but then she remembered that all the area was just as sorry. It was the ugliest part of the country she had seen. And it seemed to her that the people were like that too—ugly, sorry looking, alien.

They drove through the campground, which was completely deserted. He said he was glad they were at least avoiding the summer crowds. She told him she thought there was something sad about September—it felt as if something were over to her, always. He said he liked September, because it felt to him like a beginning. She said that was true, in a way, because of school. Then she was silent, looking out the window at the deserted sites.

Finally he pulled into a site, remarking that it was the pick of the lot, because it bordered on the only water in sight, a small creek. He got out but she crawled in the back and pulled out the bed to lie down. She had to go to the bathroom but felt she needed to rest more. It took several minutes for the momentum of traveling to leave her head. She felt too tired to cook any dinner, let alone eat it. She leaned up and looked for him, and there he was down near the creek. She hoped he would go for a long walk, for then she could nap, and wake refreshed. For now she thought she couldn't stand his presence, though she had been waiting all summer to be with him again.

But she couldn't sleep until she had gone to the bathroom. The need was suddenly urgent. She crawled out of the bus and started down the paved road to the restroom. It was cinder block, and sinister looking, so deserted and dark. She felt all at once that she shouldn't go in, she was afraid, but then she got ahold of herself and reasoned that no one was around at all, so it wasn't likely that anyone would be lurking in the restroom. She thought briefly of returning to the bus, of asking him to come back with her, never mind that it was silly, but then she knew her fear would not be something he would love in her, when in the beginning he had loved her for any and every thing. For now at least she had to be careful to do the right things—but she thought this new relation between them had only to do with the tension of the trip and having been apart for the summer. Once they were back things would be different; things would, in fact, be as they had been before.

Of course there was no one in the restroom, though it was full of insects and several dead earthworms on the damp concrete floor. It smelled foul. The only source of light came from the high narrow windows which opened outward but even in the semidark she could see mosquitoes on the wall the size of which she had never imagined.

She went in one booth leaving the door open, and urinated. It stabbed down in a short burning urgency—but there was very little urine in her bladder. She leaned over with the desire to urinate more, and realized she had cystitis, a bladder infection she had had once before. They had been making love too much, too insistently on the trip. She would have to go to the doctor when they got to Berkeley. Again her body strained to urinate and her bladder tried but there was nothing more. She sat on the toilet for a long time, too worn out to get up, with her jeans down around her ankles, her feet straddling a wet puddle on the floor in front of her. There was no toilet paper.

She knew she had to get up eventually. When she went

outside it was completely dark. She didn't know which direction to turn. The bus could be anywhere. For a moment she felt so weak she was afraid she couldn't make it back. Too many days on the road; too much traffic and speed; too many nights in strange places; too much lovemaking; too little sleep; too much junky, unnourishing food eaten at odd hours; too many days of waiting; too much love for him. But all she needed was to tell him, the saying of it all would take the raw edge away, would ease her.

She saw the light through the stakes of pine. He would be in the bus fixing supper. Walking back, she remembered a stronger, more relaxed self, and wondered why she was only a shell of that former self. But all she had to do was stop, gather herself, and call it back, for wasn't it still there?

She tapped on the window of the bus, and he smiled out at her, so brilliant in the glare of the Coleman lamp that he hurt her eyes. He told her he had everything out and cooking, and so she sat on the bed he had put back up into the seat, and watched him beat eggs in a coffee cup, dig around for the paper plates, wipe the dirty fork with paper towels. The bus seemed too small to contain his large body, and his overflowing energy. He found the hot dogs in the ice chest, and pretending that one was his penis, holding it at the crotch of his baggy pants, he crawled over the cookstove to her and rubbed the hot dog against her, saying in the manner of a beseeching idiot, "love, love." He had always been a clown. Joyfully he poured the eggs in the bubbling butter. He began chopping the hot dogs into the shiny liquid. All at once she was sick at her stomach.

What she needed was air. She couldn't breathe in the bus. As if she were just stepping out to enjoy the night, she pulled open the door and got out, shutting it behind her. Her throat kept swallowing and swallowing, and any moment she would have to lean over and heave. Her mind struggled not to picture the eggs and hot dogs. And from the bus came the sound of him, bustling and busy, manic with energy, pushing on and on and on.

She climbed on the picnic table and lay down across it with her arms to cushion her head from the hard surface. There was the black sky but she couldn't tell if it were a hard close wall, or depthless. Her heart was beating very hard. There were three maybe four days of traveling left. She breathed in short jagged breaths, and then released the accumulation of air in a long painful exhalation when she realized she had been holding her breath. Please, she said, please, please, but what was the cry for, and to whom? She shuddered all over, which scared her so badly that she sat up, her palms cold and wet when she rubbed them hard on her jeans. She talked to herself very slowly and carefully as if she were another person: in the morning, in the light, out of this place, you will feel different. It will just seem like a moment that happened, no more than that, no more than any other moment.

He sang out that dinner was ready, to come and get it, and then, more tentatively, as if he didn't quite want to know but felt he had to ask, was she all right? He had always asked that whenever he sensed the slightest sign of tension in her, and that sign of caring had always before made her instantly all right. She got up and went back to the bus. When she ate something she would feel better. He was dishing up the paper plates with the concoction, and the moment she saw it, she felt nauseous again and immediately backed out.

He wanted to know what was wrong; wasn't she hungry? She said she didn't know, she felt a little ill, wasn't she crazy after he fixed such a grand supper, her favorite, cock and eggs, trying to laugh the way she used to—it was exactly the sort of joke she had once won him with—odd. She glanced in at him and he was eating huge spoonfuls of food; she had to turn away from the way he ate. It made her sick the way he ate—shoveling it down, when her own stomach was like a stone, her throat sealed. He could always eat. He ate with a passion.

Let me know if I can do anything he said and she said she guessed not, it was probably too much traveling, that was all. It's enough to get to anybody he said but of course it hadn't gotten to him.

Feel better, he said after awhile, coming out of the bus, standing near her in the darkness, sweet, afraid, confused, resisting, closed, tender, wary. She pulled her tired body off the table and went to him, and into his arms, laid her head against his shoulder. She felt his body solid and capable there against her, and there was now no comfort in that. No comfort in his sureness, his power, his apartness. It was as if the weaker she became the more powerful he became; it was as if he were somehow draining her strength and energy and adding it to his own. But how could that be?

She said against him that she had a good idea, why didn't they take showers, it would relax them after such a tough day. He responded enthusiastically, saying he could even shave and that way he'd be ready for her tonight, another old joke. They gathered up the towels and shampoo and started off with the lantern.

She suggested he go ahead and take his shower and then he could shave while she took hers. She sat inside the women's restroom with the lantern in the middle of the floor while he splashed and sang. He came out dripping, clean, shining in the light, so handsome a young man that she watched him in something like pain as he pulled on his cut-off jeans without shorts and slung the towel around his shoulders. She had to urinate—so her body told her—but when she sat on the toilet and tried to go nothing was there except the urgency and the burning.

She took off her clothes and he embraced her in a playful way but then he held her back, naked, and a shocked look came into his face. Jesus, he exclaimed and then in a tone that frightened her more, said her name—Miriam—with something like pity, the suggestion of disaster.

She looked down at herself in the light, and all over her were huge red welts. He turned her, they covered her back too. She stared at her body and a feeling of horror came over her, she had been eaten like a piece of meat.

He thought they might have insect repellent in the car, did she want him to go back for it. She said she guessed no one had ever died from mosquito bites, and then noticed that his body was smooth and unmarked. He told her they only liked sweet things and she smiled with a quivering mouth at his clumsy way of making her feel better. She didn't want to take a shower, she guessed. Can you imagine coming here for a vacation, she joked. They both laughed but tears shone in her eyes.

He said he'd still like to shave, otherwise he'd grate her like a carrot tonight, and an image came to her mind of herself in the morning, after he and the mosquitoes had had at her, a mere skeleton, and this idea was so ludicrous and appalling that she laughed at herself and felt better. He wanted her, still.

She went back to the bus, not wanting to stay in the light with the mosquitoes, and found some repellent. She arranged the sleeping bags on the bed, cleaned up the mess he had made, was in bed herself when he returned. She held out her arms, coated in oily repellent, for him when he slipped off his jeans and eased in beside her. The katydids were screaming wildly in the pines around the bus. They held each other and talked a little about nothing, and then they were making love, and she tried to tell him with her body how much she loved him, how long she had waited, how she felt so far inside there were no words to reach it, but here, here it was as best as she could tell him. But his passion came quicker and there was the pain of the cystitis and he was way beyond her and done. He fell away. But he was still restless. She felt him unresolved there in the dark beside her. Her wide open eyes stared into the darkness and she felt the presence of the ugly pines all around them. There would be ugly birds in them. There were bound to be ugly birds.

Then his voice came to her, not as a surprise, but as something expected all along. He had been thinking about when they got back, he said. About living together. He was thinking that maybe now wasn't the time. Maybe they were too young. Maybe they weren't ready.

She lay in the dark. She knew him and knew he couldn't stop now. She agreed that they were young. It was true.

He grew more expansive. He said that they wouldn't lose each other. Not being tied together would make what they did have more authentic. They would see each other because they wanted to. Not because they were tied together. Wasn't that true?

She said that it was probably true.

He didn't want to lose her. He turned and took her in his arms. But on the other hand—there were so many people to love. Didn't she feel that way too? How could they miss out on all the other people there were to love in the world? His own heart was overflowing with love. It was wrong, he said, to limit love to one person; to leave all the others out.

She knew he was right, of course. It would all make sense eventually. She looked into the future, straining her eyes, five years from now, ten years from now, when I'm forty say—when it won't matter. When this little love affair would seem to her touching, but trivial; sweet and sad, but remote; melodramatic; a memory. There would come a time when it wouldn't matter anymore, when she would wonder how in the world it ever mattered so much at all.

She had to go to the bathroom again she said. He snapped out of his theorizing. She wasn't going to the restroom was she? Why didn't she just go right outside the bus? Did she want him to come with her? No, she would take the flashlight and only be gone a moment. She didn't like squatting on the ground, she reminded him.

She got out of the bus. It couldn't be later than ten o'clock, though it seemed the middle of the night. It was early, even though it seemed so late. She walked along the road, the light a weak circle in front of her. Her bladder burned and ached. Her vagina felt like a wound, dripping. She went in the restroom and sat on the toilet. Her bladder strained but there was nothing and the pain and frustration of it made her double over.

While she was washing her hands, suddenly she was aware that she was not alone. Something was there. It was true, her mind noted, that a person freezes when suddenly frightened. Her heart throbbed with the rush of adrenaline. She shone the flashlight into the corner. It was a huge snake, coiled, and slowly as if from a great distance came the dry shake of its rattlers. Then, in the smoothest motion she had ever seen, it flowed into a hole in the wall and was gone.

Ladies' Luncheon

Miriam is in the guest room, her room while she is home in South Carolina, with the door shut. She brought along her portable tape recorder and her Jane Fonda exercise tape, and she has on her leotard and black tights. There's not much room to do exercises, but that's okay. She pushes in the tape, and presses the "play" button, and Jane's voice, so familiar and likeable, like a good friend's really, says, "Are you all ready for your workout? We'll start by warming up."

As she's doing the neck rolls, Miriam lets her eyes sweep around the room, which is crowded with antique furniture. On the wall is a portrait of her great grandfather—the one who slept in this bed—in his Civil War uniform. His eyes are exactly centered, so he appears to be watching Miriam no matter where she is in the room. It feels a little strange to be doing exercises in front of him, but Miriam bends over, flat back, and bounces slightly to the beat, then plunges her hands between her open legs to stretch out her back.

45

There's a little knock at the door, and her mother opens it a crack. "I wondered what was going on in here," she says. "I thought I heard talking."

"Care to join me?" Miriam says. She's lying on her side on the beige rug, raising one leg up and down without touching down all the way.

"It's too late for me," her mother says, standing in the doorway. "I've got to lose some weight though. I'm going to start back to Weight Watchers next month."

Miriam's mother is short to begin with, and with the passing years she's had trouble keeping the pounds off. When her mother was young—when she had the advantage of youth—she was thin, a point Miriam keeps in mind. This past May, on Miriam's thirty-fifth birthday, her sister Linda sent her a birthday card: "One year closer to looking like Mom."

"Is everything under control in the kitchen?" Miriam asks, down on all fours, lifting her leg like a dog peeing on a fire hydrant, again and again.

"I just cut the altheas," her mother says, "and I've got them soaking in deep water in the sink. I'll arrange them right before they come." She pauses for a significant moment. "Everybody's looking forward to seeing you. They all think so much of you."

Miriam has no idea what her girlhood friends think of her. Leslie and Kay never seem to know what to ask her about her life. Maybe they're afraid of what she'll say. That thought makes Miriam laugh.

"Leslie and Kay have such nice homes, nice husbands..." her mother pauses again, "... and such nice children. I think they're both very happy."

Miriam's mother assumes that because Miriam doesn't

have any children she is unhappy, which isn't true. She's only been married a year, and the whole idea of having a child fills her with doubt.

"I'll set the table when I'm through here," Miriam says. "Is there anything else we need to do?"

"The quiche is ready to go in the oven," her mother says, "and the aspic is in the refrigerator. We just have to put the fruit on the plates at the last minute. You can put the ice in the water glasses when you set the table."

Miriam's mother has invited two of Miriam's girlhood friends, Leslie and Kay, and their mothers over for lunch. Leslie and Kay have done things the way they were brought up to do them. They've married local boys, settled down in town, had children, taken up bridge. Miriam thinks of this occasion as a Ladies' Luncheon. The point is to get together and act like ladies. Actually, the others *are* ladies. Miriam is not a lady. Her friends in Minnesota are not ladies either. They're women, and they go out for lunch. Nobody has anybody over for lunch on white linen with good china and silver.

"Is Ted still doing all that running?" her mother asks, stepping over Miriam and sitting down in the big armchair that used to be in Miriam's grandmother's house. It is rose colored, and still gives off the musty claustrophobic smell of her grandmother's old age.

Miriam nods her head "yes" to her mother's question. She's doing donkey kicks now, lifting her leg high in the air and kicking. Her husband Ted runs around Lake Harriet three or four times a week.

"Kind of makes you wonder what he's running from," her mother says and laughs.

Miriam laughs too, to herself, a short ironic snort. She

enjoys her mother's sense of humor, which often takes the form of deflating comment, as long as it isn't directed towards her.

"Don't y'all want to have any children?" her mother says. "You're not getting any younger, you know."

Miriam's not about to get into the matter of having a child. She knows her mother feels bewildered that neither she nor her sister Linda have had children. During those years when other people, like her friends Leslie and Kay, were having children, Miriam wasn't interested. She was living in California then, and none of her friends wanted to have children. Motherhood was something to postpone, or even avoid. In those days, not so long ago, they all had trouble seeing their way clear to marriage, let alone motherhood. Now that Miriam is married, she finds she might be interested, but she's not sure. Motherhood seems like such a leap of faith. Miriam has never been good at leaps. She was always the kid who had to back down the ladder of the high dive.

"Are you ready for butt tucks?" Jane asks. Then she adds in a voice that is different from her usual professional voice, a voice that is more intimate, as if she's cozying up, "These are my favorites."

"Isn't there something you should be doing in the kitchen?" Miriam asks. "I think I'll go for a run."

"Are you going out now?" her mother says. "Do you really think there's time?"

"It's only ten o'clock."

In the hall Miriam puts on her running shoes. She isn't really going to run. She's going to walk. Mainly she wants to get out of the house. When she was in the seventh grade, she'd come home from school, quickly change her clothes, and head for the woods. At a certain point in the path to the creek, two pine branches overlapped, forming a kind of gate. When Miriam would reach this point, she'd deliberately push through the soft prickly barrier, and whisper, freedom, freedom. She meant freedom from her mother.

"Are you wearing those tights?" her mother asks.

Miriam is pulling a "Hello Minnesota" T-shirt over her head. "Sure. Why not?"

"It's just that I've never seen anybody wear them like that, under shorts. Down here."

"I'll be gone about half an hour," Miriam says.

"Be careful," her mother calls as she goes out the door. "It's dangerous out there. Don't go towards the stadium, and stay out of Cleveland Park. A girl was raped there, not too long ago. Someone was stabbed."

As soon as Miriam steps outside, she knows the tights are a mistake, but she's not about to go back inside and change. She starts off briskly up Jones Street, acorns rolling and cracking under her feet, leaving bright orange explosions on the cracked cement sidewalk. She crosses at the top of the hill onto Crescent Avenue, address of the well-to-do in town.

She used to come to sorority meetings in this neighborhood, when she was in junior and senior high. They lived outside of town then, in the *nouveau riche* equivalent of this neighborhood. Her father owned a successful radio and TV business; his money was new, not old. When the business failed, and they had to sell their big house, they bought a small brick house on the fringe of this neighborhood, where her mother's friends live, the ladies she plays bridge with.

Bridge is her mother's main social activity, an outlet for her sharp, under-educated intelligence.

The girls who lived in these houses were as polished as cultured pearls. They always made Miriam feel as if her slip were showing. Usually it was. Miriam was rushed by all the sororities in the seventh grade. She joined Klaver Klub, the best one, and then, in tenth grade, Entre Nous, the second best club, having dropped a notch in popularity. She did not make a good sister. She hated to ask boys to dances. She hated initiation, because she had to swallow raw eggs. She hated initiating new girls, because she had to make them swallow raw eggs. There was actually a time in her life when she was willing to kneel down and let another girl crack an egg on her head, and pour its viscous contents down her out-stretched throat.

In a philosophy class in college, she read Plato's allegory of the cave, and immediately recognized her own life. Grow-ing up the way she did, she had been like one of those people in the cave, mistaking shadows for reality. She began to come out into the light.

She leaped into tie-dye, war protests, sexual freedom, feminism. Whenever she came home, her mother tried to find the old Miriam in the new. It was easier to put the new Miriam into the old forms, and her mother got into the habit of getting Leslie and Kay, still recognizable in a way Miriam was not, and their mothers together for Ladies' Luncheons. Some of the experiences Miriam was having in those days would have made Mrs. Craig's and Mrs. Wilson's—not to mention her mother's—permed hair stand on end. Miriam's own hair in those days fluctuated wildly from long and straight to cropped so close she looked like a new recruit.

Once when she was home, she found herself alone with

her old friend Kay in Kay's mother's kitchen. They had been in kindergarten together. Kay was the mother cat and Miriam one of the three little kittens who lost their mittens in the kindergarten play. What Kay wanted to know now that they were adults was whether Miriam had ever smoked. In junior high they had bet each other five dollars that the other one would smoke first. They had been pure young things back then, determined to outpure one another.

"Miriam," Kay had drawled. "I bet I win that bet." Kay had a beautiful broad face with startling blue eyes. She wore tinted contact lenses.

"What do you mean?" Miriam said, laughing. "A cigarette has never touched these lips." It was true. She had never smoked a cigarette in her entire life. "Of course," she added, "a little marijuana now and then, but tobacco—never."

Kay's blue eyes had grown big, as if a vision of unmitigated horror had passed before them. "Miri-am!" she had exclaimed.

In that way they found out who had outpured whom.

These days, Miriam doesn't smoke pot. She exercises, and contributes to an IRA. She's come back into the fold, more or less. She has matured, and now understands that Ladies' Luncheons are a part of her life. She's given in to them, like someone giving in to some perverse, decadent fetish. Mrs. Craig! Mrs. Wilson! She can't wait to stick her nose into the soft scent of their powder and perfume, to feast her eyes on those beautifully composed Southern faces, bespeaking gentility, kindness, sweetness, the sanctity of God and family, bridge and sherry, the beach and maids.

When Miriam gets in from her walk, her mother is in a

predictable tizzy. Where was Miriam for so long? She had better clean up the bathroom after her shower, and put out guest towels. Miriam dutifully gets out the white linen towels, which her great-aunt had embroidered, and drapes them across the towel rack. What do people really dry their hands on when towels like these are presented? She herself prefers to pull off some toilet paper and use that, rather than muss up the washed, starched, and ironed perfection of a guest towel.

Her mother has gotten the silver chest from the attic, where it was hidden, and Miriam, in her summer bathrobe, sets the table, handling with nervous care her mother's Wedgwood china and crystal water glasses. Under the bright chandelier, the table glitters and shines. Miriam stands looking at it for a long moment, as if it were art.

The guests arrive promptly at noon. Mrs. Craig and Kay. Mrs. Wilson and Leslie. The daughters have picked up the mothers, as daughters do who live in the same town, a detail Miriam notes with sorrow and guilt. Suddenly the entrance hall is filled with the sound of high cries and fluttering wings, as if a flock of pastel birds has arrived.

"Miriam, you look so good!" Mrs. Wilson exclaims in a voice Miriam would never hear in Minnesota, throaty, musical, as if words were notes to run up and down on a scale. Miriam feasts her eyes on her, former Brownie and Girl Scout Leader, chauffeur of Leslie and Miriam to endless ballet lessons, the first person ever to serve Miriam creamed tuna on toast.

"Come in, come in," Miriam's mother is ushering, flushed with pleasure.

"Miriam, my goodness," Mrs. Craig says, grabbing her. "You haven't changed a bit!"

But how can that be, Miriam wants to ask, *when all I have done is change?*

Leslie gives Miriam an elbowy hug. Even in her white ruffled blouse, she still resembles a boy wearing a dress. When they were growing up, Leslie seemed to believe she was a cowboy. She knew how to yodel and lasso. She had three horses, Mary, Barry, and Larry. Miriam rode with her on weekends, though she was a little afraid, herself, of the big brown horses. Leslie's knees were always skinned, even in high school; she always walked as if she had on boots.

Kay hangs back a little, peering at Miriam anxiously through her blue blue eyes. Her polished-cotton shirtwaist brings to Miriam's mind white gloves, the finishing touch. White gloves were once an important part of their lives.

While Miriam's mother serves Taylor's Light in wine glasses, they all sit down in the living room. Kay and Leslie get out the pictures of their children. Kay hands Miriam a photograph of her oldest girl, Shelly, in a blue satin formal, her arm looped through that of a teenage boy in a tuxedo. "This was before the Entre Nous Spring Dance," Kay explains, leaning over Miriam's chair.

"You mean to tell me Shelly's in Entre Nous?" Miriam says in amazement. She looks up into Kay's perfectly made-up face. "I had more or less assumed sororities were passé."

"Oh they're just the same as when we were in them," Kay exclaims, and laughs, and Miriam laughs too, with a feeling of surprise and bewilderment. Kay points to the tuxedo-clad boy. "Remember Jody Heard and Debbie Meshmeir? Well—that's their son!"

Leslie passes Miriam the pictures of her children, Roy, a perfectly generic-looking six-year-old, and Kevin, whose expression in his school picture resembles a police mug shot.

"They're wonderful looking kids," Miriam says, sincerely. Though she is not sentimental about children, she is moved by the idea of Kay's and Leslie's offspring. "I'm sure they give you a world of pleasure."

"Oh I wouldn't go that far," Leslie says gruffly, to show she doesn't mean a word of it. "I work so hard on their manners. I know you're a Northerner now, and y'all don't care whether kids say "yes ma'am" or "no sir" up there, but we still try down here." She laughs, and Miriam finds herself laughing too, helplessly.

Miriam passes the pictures on to her mother.

Her mother studies each picture, taking her time, exclaiming over each one, asking questions about grade levels, summer activities, lessons, talents. "Look at that Roy!" she says forcefully to Leslie. "What a handsome young man. He looks just like his daddy! And Kay, you have angels! Just angels!"

"Oh I wouldn't call them angels," Kay laughs, and throws a meaningful glance her own mother's way.

"I wish y'all could see the video tape we made of Kevin's school program," Mrs. Wilson says. "It was about the most darling thing I've ever seen!"

"Marsha won't be in a school program," Kay says. "I don't know what I'm going to do when she goes in to sixth grade. They won't let them wear shorts any more, and she doesn't own a dress."

"She'll get over being a tomboy," Mrs. Craig says, "when she discovers boys." She laughs softly, without making a sound, her shoulders shaking.

"So what are you doing now?" Leslie asks Miriam politely.

"I'm still writing," Miriam says.

"I don't know how you stand the cold up there," Kay murmurs. There is a moment of silence. "How do you stand it?"

Miriam feels all eyes turn to her.

"I don't know," she says doubtfully. "I guess you get used to it."

In the kitchen Miriam helps her mother get the luncheon plates ready. Her mother planned the menu before she got in. The quiche has two cups of cheese and a cup of mayonnaise. Miriam copied the recipe, but she knows she'll never use it. She cooks mainly out of health food cookbooks.

She carries the plates to the seated guests, who make the appropriate sounds of delight at the sight of the quiche, tomato aspic on a lettuce leaf, and the little bunch of white grapes. Miriam's stomach is growling, and she longs for a good hot roll with butter. When she lifts her ice tea glass, which is sweating, the metal coaster sticks to it, before crashing back to earth in a wild clatter of silverware.

"Shall we join hands for the blessing?" Miriam's mother says. Miriam stares at her at the other end of the table. But of course! A blessing! It's part of the script, only Miriam has forgotten, since she and her parents alone don't bother. Miriam takes Mrs. Wilson's hand and Kay's hand, feeling how cool and delicate their flesh is. It is strangely intimate, and strangely impersonal, this joining of hands. Miriam feels light-headed. What if her mother asks her to say grace! If she has to, she'll fall back on her old childhood chant: We thank thee for this food dear Lord that thou was kind to give help us to show our thanks to thee by how we talk and live.

But her mother handles the blessing, and everyone joins in for "amen"—especially Miriam.

"Miriam, are your schools integrated up North?" Kay turns to her as everyone begins eating.

Miriam puts down her fork. She's not sure she's heard the question right. She wipes her mouth slowly and carefully on her napkin. "You mean. . . I mean. . . you mean. . . " she stutters.

"Oh you don't have children so you don't have to worry about what's going on in the schools," Kay says. "It's not the way it was when we were growing up."

"Colored people have about taken over," Leslie says, as if integration were somehow Miriam's fault.

"Kay had a dilemma just last month," Mrs. Craig says. "It was Timmy's eighth birthday party, and there's this little girl in his class—let me tell you her name—Laphelia—I'll let you guess what color she is—and we just didn't know whether to invite her to Timmy's party or not."

"What did you do?" Miriam turns to Kay.

"I just had a few neighborhood kids in. That was plenty of party, believe me. Miriam, you don't know what tired is until you've tried to entertain a dozen kids for three hours!"

"Can I get anybody seconds?" Miriam's mother says brightly.

"Oh not for me," everyone choruses.

"I'll have another piece of quiche," Miriam says glumly.

"I'm in the best Bible Study group I've ever been in," Mrs. Wilson says. "We're reading the whole Bible, working our way through—of course it's taking years. We'll read a book, and get together to talk about it, and then we take home a questionnaire that asks us questions about what we've read, and we work on that, and reread and then get together again. It's very thorough."

"Mother's becoming quite the Biblical scholar," Leslie

says. "Don't get her started." She laughs, but Miriam can tell she means it.

"What book are you on now?" Mrs. Craig asks.

"Hosea."

Miriam doesn't recall a book of the Bible named Hosea. She used to be able to recite the books in order through about Isaiah or Jeremiah, but things got too difficult after that—a lot of old men's names running together, as she recalls. She had skipped the rest of the Old Testament, picking up with Matthew, Mark, Luke, and John, those names the closest thing to poetry she knew back then.

"Hosea is a curious book," Mrs. Wilson goes on. "It treats Israel as Jehovah's adulterous wife." Her sweet pink face blushes a deeper, sweeter pink.

"Miriam, tell me something," Mrs. Craig is addressing her. "You read a lot of books. Why do they put all those— bad—things in books? I don't understand it."

"I censor books for Mama," Kay says, laughing at the idea. "I tell her whether they'll shock her or not. She won't read the ones with dirty parts."

"Who censors them for you!" Leslie exclaims, and laughs heartily.

"Why, Miriam?" Mrs. Craig presses. "What's the point?"

"But... but... but... " Miriam says. "What do you mean, bad parts?"

"You know," Mrs. Craig says. "The bad parts."

"Oh. Well. It's a part of life, I guess. Part of reality. What books do you read?"

"I like historical fiction."

"Well tell us some good books to read," Mrs. Wilson says. "You read a lot. What do you recommend?"

Miriam feels herself backed against a wall. Her mind goes blank. Perversely, the only books she can think of are unsuitable: she just finished Laurie Colwin's *Family Happiness,* with its happily married protagonist having a happily adulterous affair; or how about Doris Grumbach's fine *Chamber Music,* with its depiction of lesbian love; then there's always *Southern Discomfort,* by Rita Mae Brown, where the society matron falls passionately in love with a young black boxer, and bears his child. She doesn't think that is exactly what these good mothers have in mind.

It is four o'clock, and the ladies have finally left. At least that's how Miriam thinks of it: finally.

Her face aches. The strain of so much animated good cheer.

As she helps clear the table of dessert plates, she notices that her mother is unusually quiet.

"I think everybody had a really good time," Miriam says. "The quiche was especially good."

"We needed bread," her mother says pensively, getting out two aprons from the broom closet door.

"Oh crackers were fine. Here, I'm going to wash. I had forgotten what big talkers they all are. Leslie must have a photographic memory, the way she can remember every little thing from when we were growing up." She ties on the apron and runs hot soapy water in the sink.

"Well, Leslie has turned out very well," her mother says.

"If you want to be Betty Crocker," Miriam cracks, but her mother doesn't laugh. She turns her back on Miriam. After a moment, she says, "Well, all I know is that Leslie and Kay have both done very well. It's hard work raising those children."

"Well it's certainly all they can talk about," Miriam says. "I've heard enough about children today to last me the rest of my life!"

Miriam and her mother don't look at each other. Her mother goes on putting foil around the left-over quiche and transferring the tomato aspic to a smaller dish.

"I'll tell you what I think," her mother says slowly. "I think people who don't have children are the most selfish people in the world."

Miriam goes right on washing the crystal water glasses that won't go in the dishwasher. Her face burns, as if she's been slapped. Hatred roils her blood, too dangerous to let loose. She feels how they would like to fall upon one another and, well—kill.

"Mama, do you mean me?" she says tightly. She starts in on the silverware.

"No," her mother says and stops. "Not yet."

"People who don't have children are no more selfish than other people," Miriam says hotly. She and her mother avoid looking at each other. Her mother puts the hot tomato pickles and the sweet cucumber pickles back in their jars, and Miriam washes the cutglass dish which is divided by a ridge into two halves.

"Lucille Gladstone and Eleanor McCall are the most selfish people I know," her mother keeps on.

"But Eleanor McCall couldn't have children!"

Her mother has no reply to this.

"I don't see how you can say such a thing," Miriam says. "I certainly know people who have children who are every bit as selfish. . . . "

"Look here," her mother says. "Someone got lipstick all over one of these napkins." She holds up one of the white linen napkins for Miriam to see.

"That's mine," Miriam says. She recognizes her lipstick, remembers seeing the smear during the luncheon. "I'm sorry," she says, grateful for something of little consequence to apologize for. "Will it come out?"

"I can Spray and Wash it," her mother says. "We'll soak it in cold water. You know what I do. I take a Kleenex to the table."

Miriam looks through the other napkins. Hers is the only one with a lipstick stain. How did the other women— ladies—wipe their mouths? Did they all bring a Kleenex to the table?

"I'll take it down and soak it," Miriam says.

"I'll finish up here," her mother says.

Miriam goes down the steep stairs to the basement. It is cool and dark, and she has to duck to avoid Vidalia onions knotted into a pantyhose nailed to a beam.

She runs water in the round washbasin she recognizes as her grandmother's, white with a chipped red rim. She sets the washbasin with the soaking napkins on the big vinyl-covered work table, with its old tins for Christmas cookies, an arrangement of plastic flowers faded into anemic pastels, a stack of old games, a pressure cooker, clean towels ready to be folded and carried upstairs.

Miriam sits down on the high stool. Her face feels ready to crack.

How long can she remain in the basement? There are three more days to her visit. Upstairs, she hears her mother walking around, the floorboards creaking. She could leave today. Fly back to Minnesota, escape to Ted.

But then what? The inevitable reconciliation with her mother, the apologies, the hurt feelings, the hurt. . . .

How much power her mother has! Still. Miriam would have thought she was beyond it.

She wrings out the napkins, and puts them in the washer, on gentle cycle. An odd desire comes over her. She runs cool water in the washbasin, and puts it on the floor in front of the old green couch that used to be in their den. She sits down, takes off her shoes, and eases her feet into the water. A feeling of comfort comes over her, mysterious and soothing. She is in the middle of her life. It is her life. She leans back, letting her face relax, and assume its human shape.

Two Women

The two women had not visited in quite a while. Much had happened. One small thing was that Anna had moved, and now lived in a one-bedroom apartment in a large white house which looked as if it were missing something, though Miriam did not know what, as she parked on the street and walked towards it. It was a particularly bare house in a small bare town where Anna had taken a new job. Miriam lived in the city which was two hours away, but that was not the reason why they had not visited in quite a while.

Anna, waiting, had not had time to fix her new apartment in the way she would have liked; it seemed empty. She was self-conscious that there was no rug on the wooden floor, which gave the room a cold feeling. The heat from the radiator had to be on or off, there was no in-between, and this morning, waiting for Miriam, she had screwed the knobs of the radiator on and off, on and off, and the apartment was either very hot or very cold.

When at last Anna heard Miriam coming up the stairs,

she threw open the door to show which apartment was hers, and greeted her. They did not exactly look at one another in the first moment, but they embraced.

Anna had nice manners, she immediately took coat and cap and scarf, and put on water for tea. She brought out a small plant wrapped in shiny green paper: for you. Miriam blushed a little, for she had thought of bringing Anna flowers, fresh flowers in the middle of November, but some stubbornness or stinginess or carelessness had kept her from the gesture. She didn't want a present from Anna; it made things a little more unbearable. She unwrapped, oohing and aahing, which she could not prevent herself from doing.

They had not seen each other in quite a while, and so they began talking, and all was almost gay, now, for they had missed each other a great deal. Miriam, who was a sympathetic sort, listened to Anna's dissatisfaction with the small town where she had taken the job. It all comes down to economics, Anna said: she had taken the job because of the pay and she would put up with it. But of course she had not been able to voice her complaints and criticisms to any of the people in town; they had too much invested in the place. She spilled it all out to Miriam, who laughed and understood, and once tears filled her eyes, though nothing sad had been said. Anna told how she was lucky she hadn't come to this place four or five years ago, for then a single woman would never be invited to a dinner party without a companion. All even around the table, a man a woman a man a woman, Anna exclaimed, and opened her hands in the air in dismay, humor, outrage. And women? asked Miriam. She had got up and gone into the kitchen and fixed the tea; that was how at home she felt in Anna's house. She set the Japanese teapot on the table between them in the bare living room. She

shivered when she sat back on the couch. There were no
women, Anna said, whom she felt she could be close to.
They were nice, but they were from different worlds. She
told the story of a woman in town who was twenty-eight
and a virgin, still waiting for Prince Charming. But for the
grace of God, joked Miriam, there go we. Indeed, Anna
agreed. They were sophisticated women—more so at least
than the woman who was waiting, waiting, for what could
never be.

And men? Miriam asked at last. There are two unmarried
men in town, Anna said with grim humor. And I bet they
live together, Miriam said. They laughed uneasily. Anna
went in the kitchen. I wondered if you would be hungry,
chimed her clear familiar voice—the only good store in
town is the bakery. And she brought in a plate of assorted
bakery cookies. It was so much like her, and there was
something so—lonely—in the plate of cookies, that Miriam
felt sick at heart. She had a fleeting image of herself as lover
come to call. She was glad into the very marrow of her bones
that her own life was not as bare, and she felt for a moment
the way a survivor must feel when others have perished: so
thankful, so thankful to be the one alive.

Neither of the women ate a cookie. They drank the tea,
warming their hands. Anna fussed about the heating, turned
on the radiator. Miriam poked around the apartment, admiring, complimenting, her voice a little song, no important
words—just interest, support, someone there seeing and
knowing. She let her eyes rest a moment on the bed, and
then she sang more of her little meaningless song about this
and that, so there was no silence. Once she blurted out
how nice and clean and white the walls were, had Anna
painted them when she moved in? and then in a flash she

remembered, and Anna didn't reply, as if she hadn't heard—it passed away with hardly a ripple.

Miriam looked at the cat scratching-post, for she had cats and there had been some discussion about making her a scratching-post. But she didn't have one. She didn't mention the post to Anna, for she had heard the story of how it was made, and there was that very deep secret part of her which would have liked to destroy the scratching-post and the cat and the apartment and the house and the small town and Anna. But she didn't allow that feeling to grow, it flickered as briefly and brightly as the tiniest hottest flame deep inside her and she blew it out.

They couldn't stay in the house another moment, that by silent mutual agreement. They decided to bundle up and go out for a long walk. Anna was solicitous about Miriam— did she have warm enough clothes on—look here, in the closet, at all the coats. Wouldn't she like another coat? Miriam pulled her own things, which she loved with fierce pride simply because they were hers, tight around her and declined. But she had forgotten gloves and so she took a pair—the soft worn leather ones Anna used every day.

When they went out there was absolutely no one around: that was what the place was like. It was as if they were in a movie set for a small New England town—everything was perfect and deserted. The weather was so cold it hurt, but they felt invigorated, in a nervous sort of way. At first Miriam was cold, and Anna suspected it, and said several times they should go back for a heavier coat, but Miriam said no. They visited Anna's office, which was as deserted and bare as everything else. Then they walked out of town into the country. They talked all the time of this and that, of everything almost. At last they found themselves on a small country road which ran alongside a corn field, where the stalks were broken and brittle, the color of yellowed ivory. The sky was too blue and the earth too black. Most of the trees had turned dead brown, except for an occasional shocking yellow one which stood out harshly against the background of beiges and browns and blacks.

And now they walked in silence. Anna went ahead of Miriam. They did not walk side by side, and both knew. They were silent for awhile, and finally, at last, Anna, without turning around, said Do you love him?

Miriam did not allow herself thought or feeling. To think would be to hesitate and waver and mumble and stumble and bumble, and Miriam, always, wanted things to be straight and clean. She said that yes she did, she thought she did. And made herself stop, before she went on, wavering, hedging, discussing. Yes, she repeated, she thought she did.

Anna did not turn around. She had inside herself something which was braced and which was at this moment determined to know. Still, there was something else growing sick in her. And does he love you? she asked, and still she did not turn around. She marched on at a fast pace, which was her protection.

Miriam had to hurry her steps to keep up. She took in the figure of Anna before her—her blonde hair a shade that was fragile, almost no color of blonde at all. She saw Anna's larger body and the shape of her strong legs within the wool of her slacks and the broad fragile expanse of her hips. The sight of Anna walking swiftly with great determination reached into Miriam, into a place in her as pure as sensation itself. There was something about seeing Anna, walking there, in just that way, which reached into Miriam and would not let her be.

Does he love me, thought Miriam, and then she answered, trying to be honest and straight and clean: she thought that sometimes he did, and sometimes he didn't know. But sometimes he did tell her he loved her and she believed then that it was so. Miriam kept those times as she might keep old letters or a childhood memento, or anything else useless and necessary, which she had to take out and turn over and touch every so often.

Do you love him? asked Miriam suddenly.

And Anna didn't have to think or feel: Yes, she said fiercely.

Miriam heard the fierceness and was afraid and sickened.

How do things stand between you, asked Anna.

The man had gone away. But in her heart Miriam believed that he loved her, had to love her, after all they had been through, in the name of love. After the pain they had visited on Anna, for that reason alone, he had to love her. It could not have been a mistake.

He had loved her so much when he was still living with Anna. But he couldn't leave her then, he said, and Miriam believed that to be true, she believed that Anna was weak and afraid to be alone, too dependent on the man. She had felt quite superior to Anna. No, she had agreed, he had to stay with her and help her move to this place: get her settled, paint her walls, and then he would be free to come to Miriam, his duty done.

He had come to her at the beginning of September and now in November he had gone away, to think about things, he said. For when they were finally together, he had wavered in his love; he wasn't sure. He thought, possibly, at moments, that he did love Miriam. Then doubts would swamp him; he grew silent. She had never met a man who could be so silent.

But he had not gone away for good. He had work to do in New York: that was another, more acceptable cause of his leaving. He would think about it all and he would miss her and he would return. When Miriam thought of this she smiled to herself and felt a little light-hearted and somehow benevolent towards Anna. She told Anna of her troubles, of how he wasn't sure he loved, but that she thought there was a good chance he would come back and live with her. Before she put it into words, she hadn't realized that it was actually uncertain.

I got a very different idea of things from him, Anna said bluntly. You make things sound much more certain than he does.

Miriam began to feel strange. She had the sense of something approaching which was going to strike her a blow. It was coming very slowly and silently and she couldn't tell from which direction.

You mean to tell me you've talked to him? Miriam said, and now there was a strain in her voice. You've opened things back up with him?

Anna's voice sounded remarkably the same as her own. It had the exact same tone of strain. Things were never closed between us, she said. It was never over. He promised when he left that we would see each other again. So things were never over between us.

But he hasn't seen you, Miriam insisted, a little shrill. They marched along furiously. He told me he promised that only to make his leaving easier on you.

Easier on me! Anna said in a terrible but quiet voice. Easier on him, you mean.

Yes, Miriam said. She had not allowed herself to think of Anna in the small strange town, waiting and waiting and waiting, holding onto the promise that he would see her again, that she might have another chance with him. So it was not over. But he had promised Miriam that it was over, and yet, of course, it wasn't. Miriam seemed to be filling up with something from the inside, like fog.

But, Miriam said in a smaller voice, he told me had no intention of seeing you again.

Then why is he calling me?

He's called you from New York?

Twice. He wants to see me at Christmas.

Miriam halted.

Anna did not notice, she marched on intently. She was a good ways ahead before she realized that Miriam was not behind her. She turned and saw Miriam, pale and diminished in her winter coat, standing in the middle of the country road. The two women stood for a moment, their hands in their pockets, their bodies perfectly still and alert, their knit caps pulled low over their ears, each searching the image of the other, the way one searches in a mirror for the secret of oneself.

You mean to tell me he wants to see you at Christmas?

Miriam came forward with quick long strides. She had begged him to tell her if he ever had feelings again for Anna; she had begged him for that was what she feared the most, and what seemed, when he had been with her, the most impossible. But if it were impossible, why had she had to beg him? It had been there all the time! She had talked quite a lot about honesty—they must, above all, be honest with each other, even if the truth were painful. Miriam had always believed that Anna lacked the ability to be honest with herself, and Miriam knew she herself was different.

Didn't he tell you when he talked to you that he loved me, Miriam demanded. Only a few nights ago the man had told her that he did love her. It was silly, this business of saying "I love you." Odd how she clung to it.

He called me last night. I asked him if he loved you, I felt that was the one thing I had to know, because if he said yes I'd give up—do you see.

Yes. What did he say.

He said he didn't know.

They walked on now, with a feeling of exhaustion, more slowly, though Anna still led. They came upon some ducks sitting in the river as still as stones, their heads hidden under their wings. The blue-green curve of the mallard's neck was the only color against the still brown of the river, the stark grey of the forest. The women stood and stared at the ducks.

They came to an open space of yellow brittle grass and Miriam sat down without ceremony. Her legs would not carry her another step. Anna sat a little distance away, a distance that was not natural and easy the way it would have been once. They did not look at one another. Yet they felt each other's presence very strongly, with all the associations and remembrances and fears. Each knew the other to be more attractive, more sexual, than herself. They both thought of this sometimes late at night, lying awake in bed.

But this summer, Miriam began after they had sat in silence for awhile. He told me things were almost dead between you—he was just riding things out until you moved. Anna, sitting in the sticky grass, was astonished: the summer had been almost good between them. She told how he would come home from Miriam and make love to her, Anna, with feeling. They were closer during the summer than they had ever been.

Miriam felt as if she had been slapped. So did Anna. Their faces stung. They laughed, horrified. They were angry as hornets. I thought you knew things were coming to an end between you! Miriam exclaimed. That was what I thought all summer. She was very animated. Anna was equally animated. I thought all summer he was just having a little affair with you, and that it didn't mean much. I thought *I* was the main one in his life.

As did I.

They spent the next twenty minutes telling themselves and each other that the man had not been purposefully deceitful, that probably both stories were true, if paradoxical—that was the way life was. They had probably heard only what they wanted to hear. Neither was quite sure what he had really said to her. But each was certain she had gotten the gist, certain enough to stake her life on it.

The two women felt suddenly gay: they found they hated him. They made some cruel jokes, which they enjoyed immensely, at his expense. They toyed with the idea of calling him now, together, to see what he would say for himself, but the thought died away almost at once.

What are you going to do, Anna asked at last.

Miriam broke off pieces of dry grass and pressed the brittle shafts against her glove until they broke. At some point, she said, feeling energized, powerful, proud—one has to make a decision. She felt secretly that that was the very thing Anna had failed to do; she had not been willing to end a situation which was obviously doomed. She had been quite weak in that way.

Will you end it then, smiled Anna.

And Miriam, taken aback, was all at once abashed. She smiled painfully at Anna, whom she loved at that moment for her sense of humor. Not yet, she said.

And both women smiled and nodded their heads and were full of sadness.

What in the world do we see in him? asked Miriam later. She laughed out loud, for it all seemed ridiculous, she felt almost as if she could give up this man without another thought, without a backwards glance.

Anna gave a little snort. She shook her blonde head. I don't know, she said in a sigh, and at that moment she didn't.

Their legs were growing stiff. They got up and began walking again. They had no idea where they were going. But they followed the river and that seemed as good a course as any.

The women walked together now in silence. And for a little while Miriam had the deep sense, beyond thought, that they were made of the same stuff, this woman and herself. They were in two distinct bodies but they were the same. If she were to put her arm around the other woman it would flow into her shoulder the way one's own hand flows into wrist into arm into shoulder into body.

Miriam wondered why the man had never loved Anna, for she saw that she was very fine. She despised the man for all the pain he had caused this woman, and for the pain he had caused herself. And perhaps he had loved Anna, and loved her now, though he didn't know it, or know how to say it. But he had said he didn't love Anna, would never love her, and he had said he did love Miriam. So perhaps there was a difference. But what about the times when he said he didn't know. Miriam began to feel too hot in her clothes. But why did Anna keep on with such a hopeless situation? Why didn't she just let the man go, why didn't she see that she would never be happy with him, why didn't she face herself! He had never loved and would never love her. Yet she kept on and on, she wouldn't face facts, she wouldn't let go. Why was she so weak, why couldn't she gather her life together without this man and go on, why must she cling to something so hopeless? *Why let the man hurt her so?*

At that moment Miriam despised Anna with a strange and terrible fury which shook her through and through. She said meanly in her heart: that woman is the worst kind of fool—a fool over a man.

They had come to a small arched stone bridge and walked up on it. Around them the brown crinkled leaves swirled crazily, caught in invisible whirlwinds. The sky was white as ice. It was growing colder. They leaned against the rough stone and looked into the water below them.

Can we see ourselves? asked Anna with the part of her that was whimsical.

The two women leaned over, but one of them did not lean over far enough and there was only one reflection in the stream, of a woman in a cap with her hair flowing down, her eyes, her skin, the color of water.

They walked on after awhile, and eventually they came within sight of the little village again, the one steeple spiking the sky. One of the women had found an ear of corn, with yellow kernels, like ugly teeth, which she broke off and dropped on the hard ground as they walked along. They were very hungry, they realized, but when they returned to the house they couldn't eat a bite. They drank more tea. They both felt weary, as weary as they had ever felt in their lives. It was growing late. Miriam wondered if she should leave. Once or twice she thought about her own small apartment, which was crowded with cheap furniture, and of her hungry cats who had no scratching-post because he hadn't got around to building another before he left and of the emptiness she would feel when she walked in the door. But it wasn't that.

Anna was so tired she felt she hadn't energy to breathe any more. She wanted to go in and lie down on the double bed—where he had made love to her before he went to Miriam—and sleep and sleep but not dream. But she didn't want Miriam to go. She didn't want to let her go.

At last Miriam said she must leave. They both nodded. After so many words there was nothing more to say. Miriam gave back the gloves which had warmed her hands all day, gathered her plant, and Anna helped her with her coat. They agreed they would talk later, sometime later. They stood a moment, and then they embraced again, and their backs were stiff and thin.

Miriam went down the stairs. Anna slowly closed the door.

Going across the frosty grass, Miriam knew that when she got home she would call the man to straighten things out; but that thought hardly stayed in her mind a moment. There was total silence all around, the roar of it, and stars.

When she got in the car she realized that she had left something. She searched in confusion for her bag, but no, it was here, and then the plant, but she had that too; her scarf, cap, yes, yes, she could find nothing she had lost. But the feeling, instead of fading, was swelling, opening her up inside, hollowing out a space she felt she would fall through, for something was missing! misplaced, lost beyond recall. She gripped the steering wheel and it burned her hands with cold. You fool, she chided herself quickly. It is only the gloves. It is nothing at all.

A Member of the Family

The Rathskeller was still intact, down some cement stairs in a dark alley way. We both ordered a beer, and I got a ham sandwich.

"Well, here's to you," I said, and we clinked glasses.

Later Joe said, "You know, I really wanted to go back and talk to your folks, try to explain. But Linda wouldn't let me. She said it would just make things more painful."

I nodded. My parents hadn't known what to make of my sister and Joe's separation. During the seven years Linda and Joe were married, they had come to think of Joe as family. His leaving was like a strange form of death; in some ways the emotions were just the same.

"I always thought a lot of your folks," Joe said. He cleared his throat, a habit he had developed since I had seen him last. It had been almost a year. I was home from the West Coast, as good an excuse as any, so I had borrowed my mother's car to drive up to see him. He had a new life now, that of a single graduate student at Chapel Hill, where I had been an undergraduate when they got married. Everything was as familiar and irretrievable to me as a dream.

"Do you remember that time we went skiing and Kent lost a ski?" I said.

"We should have known then he was no good for you."

"Oh, right," I said. "I remember how Linda wanted you to pick it up right after he dropped it, but you said no one could lose a ski on Lake Hartwell, and off we went. Then we couldn't remember where he had dropped it. All those islands looked the same."

"I guess your dad finally sold the boat."

"I always wondered what actually became of that ski. Whether someone picked it up. Or if it just floated onto shore on one of the little islands. It was certainly gone. Lost."

"It didn't matter."

"No."

We drank our beer, and I picked at my sandwich. I wasn't so hungry after all.

"Are you ready to go?" Joe asked.

"Could we have another one?"

Joe got up to get them. I saw how long his back was. I remembered him best of all skiing. How he would almost pull the boat around when he slalomed. He had been at his best then, in charge, happy in the summer sun on the big lake. I remembered how my sister looked skiing, timid on two skis, yet happy. I didn't like to ski. What was it I was afraid of? Hidden logs, being far from shore, deep places, and the hard fast falls.

"Here you go."

"I like beer better and better," I said. "As I get older."

For some reason this made us laugh.

"I was just thinking of something," I said. "About that time I lost my purse. I had just moved to California then, and someone stole it at a lake. I had left it on shore when I went out in a rowboat with some boys. Stupid of me, not like me at all. But the strangest part was that I simply couldn't remember everything that was in it. So I never knew exactly what I had lost. The things I did remember—easy things like my wallet and checkbook—I didn't even care that much about. But those other things, whatever they were, tortured me."

"Well," Joe said. "You probably learned a lesson there."

"I did," I said. I couldn't think what it was. I looked down at Joe's forearm. The skin was very smooth and hairless over the broad, hard muscles. He had been a Green Beret when Linda met him. In Viet Nam he had been a paratrooper and scuba diver; I don't think there was anything physical he couldn't do. The normal world, of Piedmont, our hometown, away from the air and water and jungle of Viet Nam, had seemed too small and cramped for Joe. He used to lie on the couch Linda had taken over from my parents, and read paperback thrillers by the dozens.

"I'm amazed how things keep changing around here," I said. "When I was in school it never occurred to me that they would ever put up any more buildings. I took it for granted that the campus was complete."

"Chapel Hill really is a great place," Joe said. "I'm glad I got in here."

He had finished his beer, and a girl in denim overalls brought him another. I kept looking around for familiar faces, though there wouldn't be any. The Rat was just as I remembered it, though Harry's was now an Arby's, and a new highrise spoiled the small town look of Franklin Street.

Joe was living in an old house that had been converted into student lodging, near the place I had lived. His room had the carelessness and clutter that said he did just what he wanted, and didn't care. It was a different kind of clutter from that of married life, which said that someone did care, but couldn't keep up.

He had even let his hair grow long, though he was many years too late. When they were married, he had always worn it army short. But he really did have curly hair, just like in the baby picture Linda had kept on their dresser. Had she returned the picture to Joe's mother? My mother had always told Joe to let his hair grow out, and now he had.

"You look like a hippie," I teased, for we had had a running joke. He was the family conservative, I was the family radical, though my radicalism had consisted mainly of moving to California and not marrying.

"Part of the new image."

"You certainly seem to be getting along fine."

"Graduate school was the right move."

I thought how graduate schools must be full of divorced people. They had both gone back to school.

Joe hadn't asked about Linda all day. I had prepared an answer, in case any vagueness overcame me. I would tell how she was getting along fine now, all in all. She liked her classes, had a good assistantship. I might mention the efficiency apartment she had in a low income highrise near the U.T. campus. I wouldn't try for anything beyond the facts, and besides, what business of his was Linda?

But he hadn't asked.

On my way home I had stopped off in Knoxville to see her. She had brought from home the brass bed I had slept in as a girl. Their king-size bed and the oversized furniture that went with it was stored in the basement of my parents' house. It had filled up the tiny bedroom of Linda and Joe's apartment, but of course it was meant for the future, for the house they would have someday.

We did all the usual things of a visit, going out to eat, shopping, seeing the campus and her office, driving one afternoon into the Smokies. We hardly spoke of Joe at all. Every time we came in, Linda would call out, "Where's Mama's little baby, where's my Little Sal?" and she would swoop up Sally, her big Persian cat. We paid more attention to Sally than each other. That spring, Linda's letters to my parents, forwarded on to me, had consisted mainly of anecdotes about Sally, and sometimes included a little note to my parents, from "Sal," written in my sister's childlike scrawl.

I remembered how when Joe told her he no longer loved her, had not loved her for a long time, she got dressed up and fixed his favorite dinner, leg of lamb.

"Don't have another beer," I said, when Joe had finished his third. "Let's go outside, walk around. Why waste the day?"

We climbed back up into the late afternoon light. It was a fall day, windy and blue, full of chrysanthemums. It hurt my eyes. The football game had let out. Earlier, walking down Franklin Street, we had heard the far-away shouts. Now the streets were full of jubilant people, as if the stadium had been a big cage from which they had been miraculously released.

Linda and Joe got married the summer between my junior and senior years at Chapel Hill. I stayed away that August as long as I could. I had secretly feared that no one would marry my sister. But Joe had come along at the right moment, as needful of marriage as she. I had just had my first affair that summer, and my life was taking a different turn. I was defensive, scared, and young about it. I kept to myself as much as I could. I did not believe in my mind that my life would be ruined because I was no longer a virgin. Yet I had bad dreams that my parents would find me out.

I brooded over my small role in the wedding as maid of honor. I was responsible for the ring, and when it was given to me just before the service, I felt faint with fear that I would lose it. Under my white gloves, my hands were cold and stiff. Mother instructed me that I was to assist the bride, and make sure that everything went smoothly for her. But as Linda and Joe were leaving the altar after the ceremony, her long veil wrapped around the post of the first pew, and caught there. I was fascinated by the sight of Linda moving forward and the veil clearly staying behind. What would happen? My mother jumped up and undid it. Later she berated me for not doing my job, for almost letting *something go wrong.*

Whenever I came home to Piedmont, to Linda and Joe's, I would look at their wedding pictures. How funny we all looked then, so perfect and year by year more out of date. I continued to study the glossy photographs long after Linda and Joe's interest had waned. My mother had talked me into having my hair fixed; I looked like a cross between Little Bo Peep and Irma La Douce. I remembered myself then as if I were just another person I had once known, though not well.

At the time, the wedding had seemed to me a thing unto itself, accomplished and complete. I had not understood then how everything is bound on one side by the past and on the other by the future.

A Member of the Family

We were sitting on a bench under the big oaks that shaded the campus. The sharp, sweet sting of autumn was in the air, and I moved a little closer to Joe, for warmth. He was wearing a green-and-white-striped sweater. It must have been one he wore when he was first in college. It was so hopelessly out of date I couldn't help smiling, a nostalgic joke.

We sat in silence for awhile, watching a dog chase squirrels. The squirrels made me nervous, so frantic were they for acorns, as if they knew something we did not. I was afraid a dog would catch one, and we would have to hear its high painful scream. But always the squirrels escaped up a tree at the last minute, and called down in strident mocking voices.

"Do you think it would have made a difference if Linda hadn't had that miscarriage? If you two had had a baby?"

They had tried again, there were jokes about Linda and her thermometer, for she was scientific and kept track of her ovulation on a chart. She wanted to conceive again, but could not, did not, though the doctor could find no reason why she shouldn't. Who can say what the body knows?

"I didn't want to have a child," Joe said, looking off from me. I felt very tense, very cold. "That's what Linda wanted, and I was willing but I'm glad it worked out the way it did, now. You know, considering everything."

"You mean it worked out for the best?"

"I'd say so. Yes."

Perhaps he was right. Still, I grieved for the child, selfishly. I had looked forward to spoiling it. I knew that my sister wondered if she would ever have children now. She was still young enough, there was time left, but where would she find a husband, a father? Still, she might yet have a child. She had told me about the miscarriage. She wasn't squeamish, not like me. She knew she was aborting, she got

83

out of bed, and the embryo came out into the toilet like a large messy period. There had been cramps, but nothing impossible, nothing unbearable.

"I hope Linda does get to have a child someday," Joe said. "I really wish her well. Your sister is a good person."

I nodded, shivering. It really was very cold. I no longer felt very sad. My old sadness seemed self-indulgent. Why was I always the saddest one?

Far off we saw a little knot of football players in their blue-and-white uniforms. They were walking back to the dorms, to change. I thought they would go to a party later on, and drink beer, just as they always did. That was what football players did.

"Funny," Joe said. "When I was first in school, it never occurred to me that I would ever be older than the football players. Now it gets to me. They're still twenty years old. They haven't aged a bit."

I laughed a little.

"Think how it makes me feel," Joe said.

I looked up into his face. The wind was making his eyes water. I could not tell if he were old or young, and I could not imagine how he felt, no, not at all.

"I haven't given you whatever it was you came for," he said. "Answers, understanding."

"It wasn't that."

"But you haven't really asked me anything."

"No." I shook my head. Words were far away from me, but my eyes felt very full, of the trees and grass and buildings I half remembered and had half forgotten.

"You have little feet for such a big man," I said. His legs were stretched out in front of us. He wore Hush Puppies now, which made him look tentative when he walked. They were not like boots at all.

I understood that I would probably not see Joe again. We walked back to his room. I had a long way to drive, and it would be dark when I got into Piedmont. My mother would say to me, "Well?" Later she would say, "Who would ever have believed. . . ."

There was nothing more to say, so Joe said, "I hope things work out for you."

"I do too," I said. My head felt dizzy and pained from all that had changed. Looking up at Joe, I had to remind myself that he had been married to my sister for seven years. He had once been my brother-in-law, a member of the family. He was so much a stranger to me. In that way he was just like family.

We hugged quickly, fiercely. I held him for my sister and for my mother and for myself, and then I let him go.

"You take care," I said.

"And you."

I went down the back stairs. There were already shadows in the yard. I stopped for a moment at the Fiat. I had always been afraid they would be killed in it. It had frightened me to drive in it with Joe. He was too big for it, and drove it too fast. He had never believed that anything could happen to him.

I leaned over and looked in the low window. On the front seat was a woman's scarf, crushed silk of many colors.

The Batsons
of Brown and Batson

When I was growing up, my father owned Brown and Batson, a radio and TV store on North Main Street in Piedmont, South Carolina. The store was next to the Fox Theatre, a few doors down from my uncle Jack Johnson's jewelry store. At Christmas my mother decorated the windows with reindeer and elves and artificial snow. At school my teachers always asked if my father was the Batson of Brown and Batson. They had bought a TV from him, or were hoping for a deal.

On those days after school when I didn't have a lesson or meeting, I'd get my mother to drop me off at my father's store. There was a big butterfly of colored slate inlaid in the pavement in the entryway, between the two display windows. As a child I was careful never to step on its narrow blue body, its long pointed orange wings. I knew that everyone else, customers, walked right over it. But I considered the butterfly a sign that my father's store was special.

My father was always glad to see me. He'd come striding down one of the aisles between rows of TVs. Some of them were on. He wore slippers at the store, and usually had his coat off, his white shirt sleeves rolled to the elbows. "How 'bout a coke?" he'd call out in his light, animated voice. "Are you hungry? I've got some sugar candy. How 'bout a cookie? I saved one from the cafeteria at lunch."

I'd laugh and follow him back to his desk. His top right-hand drawer was a grab bag of corn candy, cigars, a package of crushed peppermint sticks, an oatmeal cookie wrapped loosely in a paper napkin, batteries, tubes.

In the back of the store was the repair shop, dark and yet bright with fluorescent lights. It smelled of electricity. With all the broken down radios and TVs, it resembled a hospital ward in a war zone. Whit was my father's repair man. He had tattoos of anchors and snakes on his stubby hairy arms, and pin-ups on the walls. Miss March. Miss November.

My father couldn't be around a radio or TV without turning it on, or tuning it in. Customers couldn't resist what my father liked so much himself. When I was in high school, he got calls at home, just like a doctor, when someone's color set broke down during "Ed Sullivan" or "Bonanza." Sometimes he could fix the problem over the phone—a simple matter of fine tuning, or a change of antenna. Occasionally he'd make a house call. But most of the time he arranged for one of the blue Brown and Batson trucks to pick up the patient in the morning.

It was no accident that my father was in the radio and TV business. He had always been crazy about electronics. He was sixteen or seventeen years old when he first heard a

radio. Two engineers in Piedmont had a homemade trans-
mitter which they'd take on a truck to Augusta Street one or
two nights a week, to let people hear radio for the first time.
The station was WQAV, "We quit at five." My father got
himself some stuff together—an oatmeal can, some wire,
crystal—but he couldn't pick up the station in his
hometown, Marietta, so he'd get in an old Model T Ford
and come on down to his uncle Jim Trammel's on Franklin
Street, and set up in his backyard to listen.

By the time he went to the Baptist boarding school at
Tigerville, in Upper Piedmont County, he had a little one-
tube radio which he kept in a fire hydrant, since he wasn't
allowed to keep it in his room. It required a storage battery,
and some V batteries. He had to rig up a long antenna. He'd
go out at night and listen to one or two stations—KDKA
Pittsburgh or KSD St. Louis, Missouri—that's about all you
could get. The fire hydrant was just a little shack with a
wooden floor, but a lot of people came out anyway, to
listen.

He went to college at Clemson, but he was so interested in
electronics that he dropped out after his first year to take a
job repairing radios with Battery and Electric. It was also
against the rules at Clemson to keep a radio in the rooms,
and they caught my father several times, listening to his
radio. "Batson," they'd say, "take it on up to the commandant's office in the morning." "I'd take an old battery
or two and some junk," my father told me, "and seal it up
good and take it up to the commandant's office, and tell 'em
'here's my radio, they told me to bring it up here.' That happened two or three times," my father said and laughed,
"and I was still listening to my radio."

He learned a lot about electronics from a thick maroon book called *The Boy Mechanic: 700 Things for Boys to Do:* "800 Illustrations Show How."

In the front cover my father scribbled his name, William C. Batson; the place, Marietta, S.C.; and the date, January 20, 1920. The frontispiece has an illustration called "How to Make a Glider." It shows a boy standing on some fuzzy grass, inside a contraption that looks like boxy wings. Above the boy, in figure one, are some lines and measurements. At the bottom of the page, a tiny figure in boxy wings runs along a cliff and takes off—his flight demonstrated by dotted lines—flies over a train and over a river and lands safely—we're to assume—near some houses in the valley below.

Inside the book has information on how to construct wireless outfits, boats, camp equipment, kites, self-propelled vehicles, motors, electrical apparatus, cameras, and hundreds of other things "which delight any boy." Some of the delights are "how to make an Eskimo snow house," "homemade shower bath (a shower that costs less than one dollar to make)," "a practical camera for fifty cents," "how to clean a clock," and "quartz electrodes used in receiving wireless messages."

Another book my father had when he was young is small and red, rather like a journal, pocket size. It's from a cash feed company, with the phone number 2124 embossed in gold on the cover. Inside are some lined pages on which someone—not my father, since the handwriting is clearly feminine—has written some verses.

"May your cheeks still retain their dimples and your heart be just as gay until some manly voice shall whisper Dearest Will you name the day?"

"When far away in some distant land you may see the writing of my hand although my face you cannot see, won't you sometimes think of me?"

"I love you once, I love you twice, I love you next to Jesus Christ."

In among the verses are the names and addresses of young women: Miss Ava Moore, Campobello, S.C.: Miss Vasarre Turner, Cherokee, N.C.; Miss Ava Edwards, Jonesboro, Tennessee; and my mother's name, Miss Marie Homer, Texarkana, Texas, one, as it were, among many.

As it happened, after I had been away from home for several years, Brown and Batson got into some financial difficulty. How can I explain it? What can I say? There were reasons of course, factors—but what it came down to in the end was that the world was changing. A new mall had opened on the outskirts of town, and people started shopping there, instead of downtown. My father knew that if he didn't open a TV store at the mall, someone else would. He was nearing seventy, and it didn't occur to him that he was old. But it took money, borrowed money, to open another store and before he knew it my father was overextended.

I was in California, in graduate school, when the first intimations reached me.

"Exactly what is going on?" I shouted over long distance when my father alluded vaguely to interest rates, overhead, inflation—words I didn't recall hearing in my childhood.

"Now there's nothing to worry about," my father sang back in his emphatic, melodious voice. "The Big Boys are moving in"—he meant the discount houses and chain stores—"and they're hurting us some, but we'll come out okay."

On the extension, my mother was silent.

"Like I say," my father said, "Brown and Batson has always done just great! I've been in business on Main Street for forty years."

"Well, keep me posted," I said uncertainly before I hung up. I felt far away, and frightened, and in a way I didn't want to know.

When I came home the next summer for a visit, my parents were going off to the bank to sign a note. It sounded both innocent and ominous.

"Exactly what does that mean?" I asked. We were in the den, and the big color set was on. My father turned on a radio or TV whenever he entered a room. "Exactly what is a note?"

"Oh it's just a little loan to tide us over," my father said, raising his eyebrows at me, and pulling an exaggerated face. He reminded me of a child I adored. "Those boys at the bank are just dying to give it to me."

It occurred to me for the first time that maybe my father didn't know what was going on. It was a novel, and disturbing, thought. When I was growing up, he went to the store every day, he came home every night, there was money, and then more and more money when I was in high school and college.

"But a loan! The store's never needed a loan before."

"We had to sign another note six months ago," my mother said. She was wearing her best suit, from Half-acre–Osborne.

While they were gone, I wandered around the house. There was a radio or TV in every room, and I turned them on as I went along. My parents had built the house, a big brick split-level, when I was in the seventh grade. We drove out nearly every afternoon during the construction to see how things were coming along. First there was just a big hole in the red dirt, then they poured the foundation, and later we walked through an airy structure of steel beams, while my father pointed out which open space would become which room.

My mother got her formal living room with wall-to-wall carpet, and a dining room with a crystal chandelier. She picked out the wallpaper herself, Bird of Paradise. At her end of the table, under the rug, she had a little bell installed, so she could call the maid from the kitchen during dinner parties without having to shout through the closed door. Linda and I jumped on the bell so many times while the house was being built that it didn't work by the time we moved in. We didn't have those kind of dinner parties anyway.

My father got his comfortable den with built-in bookshelves for his slide carousels and *National Geographic*s. All the furniture in that room—my parents' La-Z-Boy rockers, the curved sofa—faced the big color TV. There was a guest room on the lower level and upstairs a blue room for my parents, a yellow room for my sister, and a pink room for me.

I met my parents in the gravel driveway when they came home from the bank. "How did it go?" I asked when they got out of my mother's blue Buick. My father drove a Chevy wagon, with padded green covers in back for carting around TVs.

"They gave us the money, if that's what you mean," my mother said. She looked reduced, smaller than when she left.

"Those boys at the bank are as nice as they can be," my father said forcefully. "Henry Babcock has bought every one of his TVs from me. He's got a set on the blink he's going to bring in next week."

My father changed out of his business suit into overalls and a frail cotton shirt I remembered from childhood, one with rainbow trout leaping on it. My mother took off her expensive suit and put on a model coat she had bought at an outlet of a local textile mill. Eating supper that night as we always did, at the Formica table in the kitchen, watching the portable TV on the counter, I felt reassured. It was not possible that we were about to lose everything.

We didn't talk much about Brown and Batson that winter. Maybe my parents thought my work in graduate school was demanding enough, or maybe none of us knew what to say. I could tell that trying to explain what was going on made my father uncomfortable, and I was always just as glad to let it drop. He had never been particularly versed in the business end of things. He had left financial matters to his partner Brown, and then when Brown retired, to a series of bookkeepers and accountants. What my father knew was selling TVs, and that had always worked before.

In March he decided to close the mall store. Main Street had always been good to him—he believed in Main Street—and he still believed the Main Street store could pull him out.

In the spring they called to tell me that they were going to have to sell the house.

I went to Mexico that summer. I told myself that I was going on with my own life. Those were the terms I thought in in those days.

On the pyramids of Monte Alban, on a rooftop in Oaxaca, in a hotel room in Mexico City, I saw our red-brick house on Paris Mountain: the kitchen with its matching copper refrigerator and stove; the basement rec room with the ping-pong table where Linda and I hosted teenage parties; my sister's yellow room; my pink one.

By the time I came home in August, my parents had already moved out. But my mother had saved a few things for a last trip.

The new owners, the Hardings, had spent a lot of time in Turkey. Over my mother's wall-to-wall carpets they had laid their own Persian rugs. My room was a sewing room. I kept my dark glasses on for the tour. Tears streamed down my face, and I had a bleery impression of a lot of brass.

My father offered to come up in the fall to show Mr. Harding how to turn on the furnace. My mother invited Mrs. Harding to a bridge game to meet the other ladies on the mountain. I walked out through the garage to be by myself for a few minutes. I went across the gravel driveway to my father's garden. He put in a big vegetable garden every year in the clearing he had carved out of the pine forest. White half-runners hung from the bean vines. Sweet corn was shoulder high, tasseling. My father came striding across the driveway to where I was standing. He inspected his tomato plants, which he had staked, and tied with strips from his old undershirts. He pulled a couple of the big ripe ones. "Run put these in the car," he said to me. "The Hardings won't get these."

We ate the tomatoes that night for supper. My parents were staying in the Funderburk house, a housesitting arrangement brought about through a connection in one of my mother's bridge clubs. Our own furniture was dispersed all over town—my mother's Baldwin piano in one home, the guest bedroom suite at someone else's, the dining room table somewhere else—like children from a broken home, placed with various friends and relatives for the duration. We ate off plates I had never seen before.

Part of the housesitting arrangement was that my parents take care of Shaeffer, the Funderburk's St. Bernard. Everyone was afraid of him except my father, who once a week donned an old grey plastic raincoat, put rubbers over his old garden shoes, and armed with a shovel and paper sack, went like a lion tamer into Shaeffer's pen to shovel poop. All the time he talked to Shaeffer in the silly affectionate voice he used with animals, while my mother and I hid in the house where we wouldn't have to see.

To explain to people what had happened to them, my mother said that they had sold their big house because it was "just too big for the two of them," and that they were living in the Funderburk house "until they could decide where to build." Standing beside my mother at the Winn Dixie or in Belks, hearing her deliver these lines so smoothly, I fell into a trance. I was almost a believer myself. Later, when I confronted her about it, she hissed at me, "I have to live in this town, even if you don't." Later she said sorrowfully, "I just couldn't stand to have someone come up to me on the street and feel sorry for us!"

My father went to the store every day, he came home every night, only now instead of falling asleep after supper in front of the big color set in the den, he fell asleep in the Funderburk's library, where he had put the portable TV we had had in the kitchen. Portraits of Funderburk ancestors we didn't know looked down on him.

"He falls asleep the moment his head hits the pillow," my mother confided in me, mystified. "He sleeps like a baby, while I lie awake, worrying about money."

At night I lay awake too, in someone else's bed—the Funderburk's daughter Jane's—and tried to think things through. My father still owed a lot of money. I had trouble keeping the figure in my head. Maybe there was some high paying job I could get. But the only thing I was trained to do was teach English. Maybe the thing to do was to drop out of graduate school, move home, help out. But what could I do in Piedmont? Sell TVs?

Sometimes my mother and I tried to discuss the situation. We sat at the Funderburk's dark, shiny wood table, careful to use coasters, terrified of making a ring. We had to grope for a vocabulary; neither of us had ever had a business thought in our lives. "Your father is seventy-one years old," my mother said. "I'm sixty-one. What are we going to do for money?" We sat in silence. "Everything we worked for all our lives!" my mother said. "Everything we hoped to leave to you and Linda!" Then she wept. But after awhile, she stood up, pulled herself up straight, as if she were tall—she was five feet, two inches—and said to me with a certain amount of pride, "Some people would lose their minds over this."

In September my father closed Brown and Batson. The dealers came and took away all their merchandise. My mother told people that my father had finally decided to retire.

I decided to see a lawyer before I flew back to California. It seemed the adult, responsible thing to do. I was surprised that the lawyer was my own age. I had expected someone older, wiser. It was his first year of practice. As soon as I sat down, smiled, and started to speak, I burst into tears. The lawyer was kind, he handed me Kleenex, he told me everything he knew about bankruptcy. But even as he spoke, I knew my parents wouldn't be interested. They wouldn't be able to associate that bad word with their good name.

Let us stop at this point, dear Reader, to consider the ending of this story. We know that crisis reveals character. We read a story to see what people *do,* so that we may know who they are.

So what happens to the people in this story? What do they do? Is there some dramatic finale? Does the father commit suicide? Does the mother turn to drink? Does the daughter, in her pain and bewilderment, sleep with a lot of men? (She does, but for other reasons.)

But Reader, don't you know? Don't you know these people by now?

My father went out and got a job. He took it for granted that he would work. He had always worked. He liked working.

He got a job selling TVs in the electronics department at Belks, at the mall. To explain to people what was happening now, my mother said that my father had gone back to work because he was bored with retirement.

The following summer, my parents put a small down payment on a little brick house of their own, off Augusta Street, near the house they had lived in when they were first married, before Linda and I were born, when my father was just getting started with Brown in what was to become Brown and Batson. My mother recreated her formal living room on a smaller scale, though most of the antique furniture had been sold. They turned the extra bedroom into a den, and the same La-Z-Boy rockers faced the same color TV, just as they had in our other house. The first time I visited them, I got a feeling of vertigo. All those familiar things in that strange setting. But after a few visits, I got used to it.

Eventually the electronics department closed—another victim, perhaps, of the Big Boys, as my father once called them. My father moved to toys. He showed me my first Cabbage Patch doll. When toys closed, he moved to sports. He sold Nikes and Adidas. He wore a dark blue pair of Nikes to work. Though one shoulder was considerably lower than the other, as if he'd had an internal cave-in on one side, he still looked like someone who might sprint.

One time when I was home, I visited him on the job. "Nikes. Adidas," my father said to me. "Don't you need a pair? I got 'em!"

I hadn't thought of buying running shoes, but my father brought out boxes of them for me to try on. I decided on a pair of blue-and-white Nikes. My father showed me around. He took me in the back room, where the employees hung their coats, and shared a desk to do paperwork. There were some paper lunch sacks on the desk, which my father swept aside. He sat down and pulled out the bottom drawer. "This is my drawer," he said to me.

That afternoon when I left the mall, I drove downtown to see the old store. Eventually all the department stores on Main Street had moved to the mall—Ivy's and Meyers & Arnold. Penney's. Even Belks. So many empty store fronts gave Main Street an alien and anonymous look. A discount drug store had moved into the space where Brown and Batson used to be. Driving slowly by, staring hard, I saw the in-laid butterfly. Now that I was so grown up and educated, I knew the name of the style: Art Deco.

The Reunion

There came a moment when Miriam looked across the table into Roberto's brown eyes and saw Jay's brown eyes. In Roberto's hands and gestures—Jay's. At once she felt the joy one feels in a dream, when that which is lost is miraculously restored, and at once the aftermath, when one wakes up. Roberto looked away from her, but she continued to see what she had failed to acknowledge before: Roberto's resemblance to Jay was unmistakable. Something gave way in her, she rose and went to stand at the kitchen window.

For she was over Jay, had been over him a long time. Only the sudden sensation she had just received—of *Jay*—and the accompanying rise and fall, had dislodged her sense of time. She held her eyes on the black bay below, and reminded herself that she was bored by broken hearts, especially her own, and no, she would not have this feeling, of sadness and sickness, of remembrance of things already long gone and unfinished which could never be finished. If things would not be finished by themselves, you put your will to them and made them done.

She turned, suddenly self-conscious. But Roberto wasn't looking at her, and so she stood studying him. His profile was Mayan. Perhaps his ancestors in Mexico had lived in the mysterious city of Palenque, had run silently through the jungle where the insects screeched like the ghosts of even more ancient ancestors. She returned and sat across from him at the table. They had not spoken since they got out of bed. But even in the silence there was something shared, for didn't they feel alone in the same way? If lovemaking could bring you close, it most assuredly could fling you as far apart as anything she had seen. She wondered if she and Roberto could ever regain the old comfortable simplicity of affection, friendship, and camaraderie they had shared prior to this evening. She left the silence, for once they had understood each other well enough to accept the loneliness of each other now.

It was loneliness then which drew them back to bed. She lay on her side and he curled around her with the warmth of an animal. They were over trying to be lovers. It was dark in the bedroom, and she felt pressing against the wall, but held at bay, the big bright city outside. She breathed in the musky smell of Roberto, and herself, and her body, so stiff and full of anxiety, began to warm and almost relax as Roberto cupped against her. There was not the tension of another unlike oneself, a lover, the other half of the magnet, pulling.

And it was dark and with her eyes open it was dark, there against the warmth of Roberto holding her in the dark. She had not felt so sad—such a brimming full sadness—in years. She had thought herself over that feeling, leaving it behind with Jay, four years ago now. Her body seemed to remember with a physical pain the way he had held her, just like this! They had slept all through the night curled so, waking to make love. She remembered a time when love was the easiest thing in the world.

It was the old easiness she had sought this evening with Roberto. There had been several men since Jay, good men whose company she enjoyed, but there was a point beyond which she did not go. Desire, once a sure strong force, had become elusive, tentative; she was afraid. She had gotten to know Roberto over the summer at the hospital where she had a CETA job assisting the overloaded social worker. Roberto was working in the lab before beginning medical school in the fall. Miriam had liked him immediately, for he was reserved and dignified, and though he was only twenty-two (young enough not to be a threat), he was more adult than most people she knew.

Tonight she had invited him to her apartment, but she had forced things. She could not stand to let the delicate feelings of affection, teasing, and tenderness which exist between people who will eventually make love ripen and swell—for what if those feelings died? She had dragged her desire, as fleeting as a fish, unwilling to the surface, forced it on them both, and made love, the easiest thing in the world, impossible.

She told him in the dark that she didn't know what had gotten into her, and he said in his charming accent, nothing, that was the trouble, and they laughed together, in the same boat. He said he hoped she didn't think it was like this all the time with him, and she was touched by the simple anxiety in his voice, how nerve-wracking a single instance of impotency could seem, even though they had read enough books. Oh no, she reassured him too adamantly, so that what should have been simple didn't quite dissolve between them. She had no idea whether it happened to him all the time or not. And why should he tell her? She had no intention of revealing herself to him, as she at that moment was feeling: damaged.

If Grant and the gang could see us now, she said to shift gears, speaking of their co-workers at the hospital. They stared for a moment at this picture of themselves, all their grandiose bravado gone off like a dud firecracker. There was something in it that made her smile. Bodies and souls so recalcitrant, inoperative. Roberto, though he was young, always appeared so sure of himself, as if he had been a man for years. And she supposed she appeared equally sure of herself in a different way—out there in the real world. Despite her lack of formal training, she had developed a reputation at the hospital as someone skilled in seeing people through the worst. Stepping in in time of trouble, into the heart of pain and sickness and sometimes death, she became more than herself, older, wiser, and sometimes, alight with love. She was actually two different people—her professional self and her personal self, and more often than not, she lived only in the self that gave to others, neglecting to minister to herself.

"This would ruin our images for sure, *loca*," he said into her hair, nuzzling to tickle her a little, for now there was something as nice as humor between them, even if they themselves were the joke. In unison, by unspoken agreement, they turned and she embraced his back, molding herself to him, and then, before she could help herself, she dreamed for a moment that she was holding Jay.

It was quite remarkable how something indefinable, but physical about Roberto brought Jay back to her, as if not the mind but the skin, the muscles, remembered and longed and regretted. It made her sick to think that she might be trying to find Jay again in Roberto. But wasn't it a common thing to see an old lover in a new? She decided to tell Roberto, casually, that he reminded her of an old boyfriend. Admit it, put it out in front of them. Laugh about it and have done.

"Jay," she began, and the name hung in the air for a moment like a bright flare, illuminating the dark, holding its incredible shape, holding, holding, and then it crumbled and all was black again. For a moment she doubted that she had actually spoken it. But she felt shaken. Her usual grasp on herself seemed strangely numb.

"Jay!" Roberto repeated with mock indignation. "Now you can't even remember my name. What cruelty, Yolanda!"

Miriam punched him, but for an instant she wasn't sure, perhaps he had called her by the wrong name by accident too.

"Who is this Jay you mistake me for?" he asked, and when she said "nobody," strangely, the marrow of her bones seemed suddenly to ache.

"He is your husband?" Roberto asked, hopefully she thought. "No," she said. "Your boyfriend?" he asked, adding dramatically, "who doesn't know we are together, like this, at this very moment. . . ."

"Nope."

"Your brother?" and this time she laughed.

"An old boyfriend," she said. So much for language. Lover was too coy; friend completely off the mark. And he had not been husband, that definitive term. "It was over a long time ago. I hardly ever think of him now."

"If you were married that would excite me," Roberto

said. "I have a thing for married women. It is more erotic."

She considered this possibility. "You find the idea of getting shot titillating?"

"It adds something," he laughed, stroking the smooth swell of her stomach. She liked Roberto. Maybe he liked her.

"I will tell you something," he said. "There is this woman, in the *barrio*, who is married to this friend of mine. They are all married," he added. "I see her when I am home. And always there is this—feeling—between us, you know, a sexual thing. We want each other so much. I feel it all over when I am around her, and I know by the way she looks at me she feels it too. Sometimes when we are alone in the kitchen or somewhere—for just a moment—we kiss passionately. And there are others—all married. I have a thing for married women."

"Interesting."

"I haven't had a real girlfriend for a long time. A lot of women, but no one special. I don't want to get into the same fix over a woman as I did with this woman I lived with. I don't want to do that for a long time again."

As if to prove his point, very gently he unwound himself from her. She could hardly bear the separation of flesh. She thought of the monkeys in Harlow's experiment who had surrogate instead of real flesh-and-blood mothers. What one needed was another body, for comfort, for well-being. She curled around herself to fill the void.

Roberto sat for a moment on the side of the bed. Then she heard his feet padding to the bathroom. She waited in something akin to pain to see if he would leave. But in a moment he was back with her, and she clutched at him like a newborn thing. He held her tight and laughed, stroking her hair.

Then he propped up on a pillow, and lit a cigarette in the dark, and for a few moments he smoked it contemplatively, holding her against his chest.

"I will tell you a story," he said. "One time when I went back to Mexico. I went to Acapulco. I must have been sixteen, seventeen, I forget. It was in the summer. I went on the beach, and there was a very beautiful woman. I don't know what happened. We started talking. I think she started talking to me, but who knows. There was between us, you know, a lot of excitement. We went to a hotel and I paid twelve dollars for a room. Then when we were in the room, she wanted money. Money! I paid, but then I couldn't do it. Never before had it not worked." He put his cigarette out, and it was completely dark again. "Everything in me felt like it was boiling. Money!" Then he put his arm around her waist, and they slid down into the bed, wrapping around each other.

"Well, it wasn't your fault," she said into his neck. "I mean tonight."

He shrugged. "It doesn't matter."

"You know the way we are together around the hospital. I just thought it would work, that we'd be good together. I wanted it to be easy. *I* wanted to be easy."

"You are a very serious person," he said seriously. "You don't have to apologize for that. I like you fine, Miriam. I want to stay here with you tonight. We are good friends, aren't we?"

The dignity and kindness of Roberto. Sometimes he accompanied her on her visits to the old or frightened, the sick and dying. And always, that dignity and kindness. People responded to Roberto as they might a priest, someone capable of blessings. He was a very handsome young man, tall and dark and slim. He came from a large poor family and always carried around with him, unspoken, realities which set him apart from most people she knew.

"I want you to stay," she said, and tears suddenly came to her eyes. Unbidden, as if on cue, a long ago voice in her recited: "Abide with me: do not go away...." and there it was again, all at once, the poem they had loved, she and Jay, the Delmore Schwartz. She hadn't thought of it in a long time. But it lived in her still. It had never died.

> Abide with me: do not go away,
> But not as the dead who do not walk,
> And not as the statue in the park,
> And not as the rock which meets the wave,
> But quit the dance from which is flowing
> Wishes and turns, gestures and voices,
> Angry desire and fallen tomorrow,
> Quit the dance from which is flowing
> Your blood and beauty: stand still with me.

But then the other voice:

> We cannot stand still: time is dying,
> We are dying: Time is farewell!

And the old dream:

> Stay then, stay! Wait now for me,
> Deliberately, with care and circumspection,
> Deliberately
> Stop.
> When we are in step, running together,

The Reunion

Our pace equal, our motion one,
Then we will be well, parallel and equal,
Running together down the macadam road,
Walking together,
Controlling our pace before we get old,
Walking together on the receding road. . . .

The receding road, and she saw them again, there they were, she and Jay, "Chaplin and his orphan sister." Four years had passed! She had to count on her fingers, find the familiar road posts, the landmarks of time. I lived there then, I was doing this and that, I was how many years old. And she hadn't seen him since. Somewhere he was going right on with his life, all the details unknown to her. It was simply unbelievable. Yet she had accepted it, or so she thought, for a long time. But he had come back now for a visit, untimely ghost, and tonight it seemed that what remembered and mourned was not even her memory, her brain, but her body, her blood.

"You are crying, Miriam," he said, for indeed she was. "You are so sad."

"I never cry," she said, crying harder. "I haven't cried in years."

"I hope it's not me. I have disappointed you."

"It isn't that. I'm afraid it isn't you at all. I'm sorry. I don't know what has happened to me." She could have added that she felt all torn up inside, but the words would not come out. Her throat ached with the effort of stopping the crying, but still the tears flowed. She was amazed. In a very short while she was actually sobbing, curled up on her side as if all the sorrows of the world were hers alone. She was used to counseling everyone else to cry, to let it out, but she had never taken the advice herself. She had never cried over Jay, never. At the time she had told herself it was a point of honor not to let it hurt her so, but in truth to grieve would have meant admitting her loss, and she would not do that. But now, she acknowledged, something has caught up with me. She was painfully conscious of Roberto lying beside her, uncomfortable as hell no doubt. Well, it couldn't be helped. She had given others permission to weep—their faces flashed through her head, a myriad of them, their losses incalculable—and she had let them use her shoulder, and feel better for it. So she gave herself up to it. For a long moment she had no idea what she was crying over, for the sorrow seemed larger than her own life, and she cried for it all. When she was through, she sat up, turned on the bedside lamp, found a Kleenex, and blew her nose. The storm of emotion that had seized her had passed, and she too actually felt better. Around her was the debris, broken branches, flooded streets, a sense of survival despite gigantic odds.

She smiled at Roberto in a weak way. "I can't believe it," she said, shaking her head.

"You are all right now?" He had propped himself up in bed, and was lighting another cigarette, as if settling in. She would have been out the door if she were he. She stared for a moment at his chest, bare, and how beautiful it was, both boy and man, with the sculpted contours one saw on Greek statues, and as hairless.

"Aren't you glad I invited you over for dinner?" she said. "You didn't know what I had planned for dessert." She propped up beside him, he put his arm around her, and she leaned back, exhausted but calm. They lay in silence for quite awhile, and she went over again the way it had been.

The Reunion

It had ended with a phone call, that simply. Jay had called to say he wouldn't be seeing her anymore; he didn't even come to tell her to her face.

She had met him in graduate school at Berkeley. At first she hadn't even been interested in him; it was he who fell in love with her. She hadn't taken his attraction seriously; it was flattering, that was all. But in time things changed. It was she who loved, and he who became uncertain. Miriam finally had to force the issue. He had to commit himself, be with her, or end it. For quite awhile he was in doubt; then he decided that he did love Miriam, had to be with her. But in the end, at the final moment, he couldn't do it. They had never been in step, though they had tried to match pace God knows, and in the end some kind of truth had made itself known.

When she answered the phone that day she was afraid something terrible had happened to him. A picture came to her mind, of him in the hospital, their future postponed indefinitely. "I have bad news for you," he said. Odd how he put it. Her bad luck. "I won't be seeing you anymore." Fine, she had said. Fine, fine, fine. All she wanted was to get off the phone. She had never wanted anything so badly as to hang up. The phone burned her hand like dry ice, she couldn't shake it loose. She hung up, and it was exactly like a physical blow, she was that stunned. She could not come to her senses, she wandered around the apartment moaning like an animal. For a year she had felt so much anger towards him that it had stopped every other feeling. She was determined that he wasn't going to stop her in her tracks. She clinched her teeth, she did the best she could. In time she got the job at the hospital and she went to work every day, she did a good job. She never saw him again, they never spoke again. He thought that a phone call ended things, but things went on and on. She knew that they did for him too. She knew him, and she would go on and on for him. But she reasoned. It had all been for the best, though that was never the point. It was for the best that they not live together, marry. In time she put her will to the voice that had tried to shout at him across time and space, and reduced it to a whisper. But something hadn't run its course. Something had been cut off too soon, it had a jagged raw edge that cut like glass. It cut her and cut her. It was like a shard of glass she had swallowed which moved around inside her cutting her up. She felt like spitting up blood.

Roberto had fallen asleep. He was breathing very deeply, almost snoring. She looked at the clock: two a.m. Trying not to wake him, she spoke softly to him, asking him if he didn't want to stretch out, he would get a crick in his neck, and obedient as a child, sound asleep, he sat up, fixed his pillow, and stretched out full length in bed, even claiming some of her side.

Miriam turned off the bedside lamp. Her eyes felt hugely dilated. She lay down, but couldn't help twisting and turning, she wrestled with the covers, tossed them up in the air, letting them settle in what she hoped was a restful pattern. She crept over to the edge of the bed, and hung over the abyss. Her body felt exhausted, but her mind was as bright as a searchlight, and as persistent. She concentrated on the little vial inside her that would dissolve to release the chemical that allowed one to sleep, but it had the shell of a time capsule. Where were all the motorcycles, sirens, leftover firecrackers, and mating cats she normally slept in spite of? It was quiet as night. So quiet she could hear her own blood ticking. What felt like an air bubble passed through her heart. She lay in stiff alarm, fearing a heart attack. She felt her breasts for lumps. Apparently she would survive yet one more night.

But at last, without enjoying it, she slept. Still, never one to leave well enough alone, she dreamed. She conjured up a painful dream scene in which she was confronting Jay with all her bloody pain, telling him at last how he had hurt her. Only Jay said, it wasn't like that at all, it's not the way you remember it, you've made all this up. You didn't have to be so hurt.

What kind of dirty trick was this! To not only hurt her, but deny that he had hurt her! It was outrageous. She was so shocked she woke up.

And there she was, a million light years away, in her own bed, with somebody—it was an effort to think who—fast asleep, snoring!—beside her. For a moment she had felt completely disoriented, could not remember where she was in her life. There was the draining away of anguish; she remembered the dream.

Here was a new variation on the theme. At last she had her chance to confront Jay, only he hadn't gotten it, he wouldn't take it. If she saw him now she wouldn't be able to present him with that platter of pain, saved for him so long, served up like the head of John the Baptist. Who's this, he'd say, no thank you, I've already eaten. We were different people then.

The time for words had passed. Time had passed. Even her pain—so much of it—had passed. Only on an aberrant night such as this, when she was having a hormonal attack or something—had he come back briefly to torment her in the old dear familiar way. But he would not be staying. Time itself was prying him from her. During her waking hours it was hard to concentrate on him any more. Weeks went by when he didn't even cross her mind.

She got out of bed and went softly on bare feet to stand at the kitchen window. She wanted to see the bay. It was invisible at first, but slowly it reared its black back in her vision. She had taken the apartment for the view. That first year, alone, she had stared at the bay as if it might hold some message, some metaphor, but it was only itself.

She wanted to stand here now and lose herself but she could not. She could not stop long enough. She returned to bed, to the warmth of Roberto. There were so many endings to love, too many. It ended again and again and again. Sad to forget; painful not to care so much anymore. She had willed it to be over for her a long time ago, and it was odd really, how long it actually took, yet how inexorable—in spite of herself—the process was. But even this coming to the end of her pain had its own price. It was another kind of loss, with its own grief, its own regret.

Sleep was like dark water she waded into and was swept away. Deeper yet she half-awoke to the warm smell of the man beside her, and the pressure of someone's (her own?) desire. Still she flowed, carried along on the current. Roberto stirred and turned and embraced. She found his mouth with her own, hungry for it, hungry through and through. She stroked his hair tenderly, dreamily. He was slipping his hands under her gown, large warm hands that wanted her. There was a long low wailing of longing rising in her, like the wailing of women waiting outside the mines for their men to be brought up, women waiting in the towns for the bodies to be brought home. Feed me. Roberto slipped his hands under her to raise her to him. She tried to summon Jay again, to have him one more time, to be true in some dreamlike way to the memory of him. But Roberto was insistent, himself. She felt them both struggling in her arms, the past and the future, and she wanted it all. The water rose, a wave of grief crested in her, for Jay whom she would never love again, for herself who was gone, that young woman who had loved him and could love him no more. She felt it all commingling in her, she wanted to stop time and hold it all forever, to stop, but she could not hold on, she had to let go, and her body overflowed. Tears poured from her eyes, ran down the tracks of her temples and were diverted by the little dikes of her ears. Roberto slumped on top of her, and she was patting and rubbing his back, rubbing and patting, her mind blank. They lay that way for a long time.

But eventually someone had to go to the bathroom. They stirred, pulling themselves apart like suction cups. They laughed at the size, or rather lack of it, of his sex. He padded to the bathroom, and sat down like an old man. Miriam heard a sigh and the toot of a fart. When she went in the bathroom he was standing at the mirror, and she had to laugh. He looked as though at any minute he might beat his chest and strut around like Mary Martin singing "I gotta crow. Ur ur ur ur!"

Their eyes met in the mirror and they smiled shyly at each other. They stood arm in arm, admiring their reflections— what a fine looking pair! She studied Roberto—his shaggy black hair, the spray of golden freckles under his eyes she had never noticed before. What was it about him that had reminded her so of Jay? She couldn't remember. And who was that other familiar stranger, that smiling woman with the rosy cheeks?

Hello, she said. Hello, hello.

She awoke in the morning to the sounds of a madman in the kitchen, clamor of pots and pans, sputter of Mr. Coffee machine, insane whistling. She stretched from head to toe, spoiled and petulant as a satisfied woman.

"Are you crazy!" she yelled. "It's Sunday morning. Normal people sleep late."

Roberto came and stood in the doorway in his shorts. "You will sleep the day away, Miriam," he smiled. "It's almost eleven o'clock."

She fell over backwards and stuffed his pillow over her face. "Eleven o'clock!" she mumbled. "I'm up," she said, not moving. But in a moment she did get up, and went to stand at the kitchen window, to see the bay. He came and stood behind her, and put his big hands on her. She felt the thrill of the whole day stretching before them, time to savor and squander, to spend.

Over breakfast Roberto was expansive. The history of his family, all twelve of them, his plans for medical school in the fall.

"We need much time to talk," Roberto said. "I have much to tell you. Sometime I will tell you about the young lady I lived with. It is a love story. She loved me very much."

"That's what you say."

Roberto laughed, but then he added thoughtfully, "I wonder what her side of the story would be."

Miriam looked at Roberto. His eyes were cast down,

seeing something she could not see. She felt around them a presence as palpable as the past.

Roberto returned to her and she met his brown eyes.

"But that is all over now," he said, smiling. "I hardly think of her at all any more."

Miriam said she knew just how true that could be.

At the Beach

This winter, when it was twenty below in Minnesota, with a windchill of minus sixty, I wrote my sister Linda, who lives in Tennessee. "I really enjoyed getting your letter yesterday," she wrote back, "and reading about the beach."

Our parents took us to the beach every summer when we were growing up. We'd rent a motel room along the strip at Myrtle Beach. The four of us—my mother and father, my sister and I—would walk across the black asphalt highway which was so hot it would blister bare feet. We'd wear rubber flip-flops and carry bright striped beach towels, straw hats, buckets and shovels, suntan lotion, T-shirts for Linda and me to put on when our shoulders started to burn. Our mother always wore a black bathing suit, one piece. She was fleshier than our father, in the way of women, and her legs were tan from the knees down but her thighs were white, very white. They were soft with no suggestion of muscle, and there were bruises where she had bumped into something or other. Our father wore trunks, dark red or navy blue. His legs were white and skinny. Linda and I would giggle at them behind his back; they were as thin and shapely as a girl's. Linda and I wore two-piece bikinis, pink and red, yellow and orange. We'd lie on the beach until our skin seemed about to ignite. Then we'd run into the ocean.

"Your letter brought back so many memories," Linda wrote. "Especially pleasant was the time we rented floats and had such a good time in the water. I remember so often that time a huge wave caught us up and lifted us so high and then the wave broke and we both really hit the sand and I don't remember getting hurt but just laughing and laughing."

My sister is three years older than I am and can remember more things from our childhood. Grown-up, married, and living in Minnesota, I read this part of her letter over and over—"the big wave, the laughing and laughing." We must have had fun.

It is summer now and Linda and I are on vacation together. We are at the beach. Our parents made reservations for us at a motel they know, for while Linda and I have grown up and moved away, and neither of us has been to the beach for years, our parents have continued to come here each summer, and so have kept up on where to stay.

We almost didn't make it to the beach. One of my sister's cats got sick and nearly canceled our trip. When we were growing up, I was the one who was crazy about cats. Linda was allergic to them. It is not at all clear that she has outgrown her allergy. Her house in Tennessee has an elaborate air filter built into the heating and cooling system, which pops electronically all the time, burning up cat hair. She got her first cat when she got divorced and went back to graduate school. Now she has a doctorate in education, a high paying job in a tiny school district in Tennessee, and six cats. She talks about the cats as if they are people. This spring, when we were planning our trip, if she'd start talking about the cats, I'd change the subject.

We met at our parents' house in South Carolina. I had looked forward to all of us being together again. I pictured us around the dinner table, reminiscing over good times, eating my mother's fried chicken and cream gravy. Instead, that first night home, the four of us stood around the sick cat, peering at it. It lay on the couch on a towel, my mother's suggestion. It was a pretty white cat with yellow mixed into its fur. Linda sat down next to it, and stroked it, talking baby talk: "That's all right, Pumpkin, you'll be all better tomorrow." She wasn't wearing any make-up and her face looked pale and pockmarked. She still gets big angry-looking pimples. Linda was the girl in high school who had the worst complexion. Her teenage years were a round of dermatologists, sun lamps, tubes of sulfuric smelling ointments, pancake make-up. It was not the sort of thing you could cover up.

"I'm so worried about Pumpkin," she says to me, emitting a high, thin whistle with the breath. She wads a Kleenex in her hand, and inhales deeply from a small bottle of Primatene Mist.

"We don't have to go tomorrow," I say to her.

"I don't see why somebody who's allergic to cats would want six of them sleeping on her bed," my father says.

"I don't have to take that!" my sister says. She runs from the room, and we hear her feet pounding up the stairs.

My mother turns to my father. "You know it only takes one word from you and she'll drive back to Tennessee tonight."

My mother follows my sister upstairs. She will comfort her, talk her into staying.

"What did I say?" my father asks me. "I don't understand Linda." He goes and sits in the La-Z-Boy rocker and begins to read the evening paper. He gave me my first kittens when I was seven. I came home in my Brownie outfit, and there he was in the backyard with two black kittens in a cardboard box. We kept them outside because of Linda's allergies. She couldn't touch them without itching or sneezing.

Upstairs my mother says to me, "Do you think she's getting an asthma attack?"

I take a step backwards. "She hasn't had an attack in years," I say, which is true. "She's outgrown it."

Once when we were little, our parents were out for the evening and we were staying with a babysitter. We watched a TV program about a little boy who had an asthma attack and died. That night Linda started wheezing so badly she had to be taken to the hospital.

"I know a woman, a friend of mine," my mother says, "who had an asthma attack and was dead in five minutes—before she could get help. In her own home."

I think of my sister in the next room, breathing shallowly from the top of her lungs, trying to relax. I cannot understand why my mother would tell me such a thing.

I open the door to Linda's room and go in. She's lying on top of the covers. She has been crying. "I don't want to ruin our vacation," she says to me. "You've come so far and spent all this money."

"We'll still go," I say. "We don't have to leave tomorrow."

The dark roots show at the edge of her blonde hair. She started dying it when she was a teenager. It used to embarrass me to have a sister who dyed her hair. That was in the early sixties, when Marilyn Monroe was still alive. We'd go to see her movies on Saturday afternoons. *Some Like It Hot. Gentlemen Prefer Blondes.*

"Will you give Pumpkin his pill?" she says to me. "I don't think Mama can do it."

I go downstairs and find the cat still on the couch. It seems to be watching TV. My father is asleep in his chair, snoring softly, his legs crossed, his foot going up and down, his way of showing us he isn't really asleep. The pill in my fist, I sit by the cat and stroke it to gain its confidence. It purrs sweetly when I touch it, that responsive. Please don't die, I beseech it silently. I don't want to be around when one of Linda's cats dies.

When I tip back its head, and try to insert a finger to open its mouth, it comes to life, bolting off the couch. It runs into the guest room and hides under the bed. I crawl around on the rug, first on one side of the bed and then the other, trying to reach it. I poke at it with a coat hanger, and finally corner it when it runs into the bathroom. I hold its head very firmly, so it can't move to the left or right. I pitch the pill so far down its throat it has to swallow. But in the process, it gives me a long red scratch on my arm.

That night in bed, I lie awake remembering what I thought I had forgotten. How I used to lie awake as a child, listening for my sister's breath. I was the guard, the gatekeeper. When we finally moved to a bigger house, and I got my own room, I was relieved. I shut the door. Now in the dark, in our parents' house, we are all together again and my sister's breath whistles in the room next to mine. My own breathing feels unnatural. It feels as if something is sitting on my chest. When I dream, I am at the beach. I am on the long pier that stretches over the ocean. I have come a long way to get here. A fisherman pulls a fish from the sea. It is small and silver. It flops about on the grey planks of the pier, gasping, drowning in air.

In the morning the cat is missing. Then my mother finds it in the breakfast nook window, watching sparrows on the chinaberry bush outside. During the night it has eaten a whole can of catfood, and so my sister and I can go to the beach.

Linda has had a good night's sleep. She has washed her hair and fixed her face. She is no longer wheezing. In a little while it will be hot, and my mother will put down the kitchen window, close up the house, and turn on the air conditioner in the den, which will cool the downstairs. But now the morning air is fresh and wonderful, it fills the house.

Our parents have packed a cooler for us to take. We will fix breakfast and lunch in our motel room, and at night we will go out for seafood. The cooler has the food of our childhood—white bread, pimento cheese, peanut butter, milk—and the drink of our independence—beer, and tonic for our cocktails before we go out for dinner.

Over a breakfast of grits and sausage, our parents tell us all the good places to go out to eat: The Captain's Table; Neptune's Cove; Windy Hill Inn. Our father is particularly nice to Linda and she is particularly nice to him. "I didn't mean anything last night, Honey," he says to her. "You know I wouldn't hurt your feelings for the world." Tears brim in his blue eyes, something that happens more frequently now that he is old. Linda's voice sounds broken when she answers him, "I know it, Daddy."

Our father has bought two jars of nuts. They always have nuts with their drinks before they go out to eat at the beach. He holds them behind his back for us to pick left or right, the way he did when we were children. I get the cashews, Linda the peanuts. "You always were the lucky one," she says to me.

When we leave, our parents stand in the driveway and watch us go. They look very small to me and old.

We drive slowly out of our hometown, Linda at the wheel of her good Buick with air conditioning and an AM/FM radio, our clothes and food in the backseat, money in our pockets. "Who would ever have believed," Linda says, "that we'd grow up and have only two weeks a year for vacation. We're actually people for whom a vacation is a luxury!" She shakes her head in amazement.

The highway to the beach is straight and once we are on it, there is nothing to think about except the past and future. The land turns flat, and gradually changes character, becomes more tropical with swamps of live oaks draped with Spanish moss. We talk about our lives, our jobs, we listen to the radio, I doze a little, we change drivers.

It was on this highway, on one of our trips to the beach when we were children, that Linda threw my baby blanket out the car window. I was to start first grade in the fall, the blanket was nothing but a tatter, it was past time for me to give it up. Linda was so fast. One minute I had the blanket, my babyhood, securely in hand, and the next minute it was flying down the highway behind us, flapping like a bird. I regarded my sister on the seat beside me for a split second. I was impressed by the magnitude of her gesture; I hadn't realized she had the guts. Then I burst into a tantrum of anger, outrage, and loss. I was inconsolable for a few days, then I got over it. Perhaps I was secretly relieved.

"How do you think Mama and Daddy are getting along?" Linda asks.

"They seem pretty good to me."

Linda nods. "If they can just keep their health."

"Just so you take them in in their old age," I say and grin. It's a running joke, a hot potato we toss back and forth. Neither of us can imagine taking them in.

Linda gives me quite a look. "Oh, great," she says, shaking her head. Then she says, "You know, it's so funny. When I was married, I felt responsible for them, because I was married and settled, and you were single and free and couldn't be bothered. Now that you're married and I'm single, I feel responsible for them because you're married. . . ."

We look at each other and then we start laughing. We laugh until tears fill our eyes. We laugh until it hurts.

When we arrive at the beach and find our motel, it is identical to all the beach motels we have ever known. It is two stories, and built like an L around a swimming pool overcrowded with people. I am shocked by how brown the people stretched around the pool are. They're baked as brown as loaves of bread. I'm still very white from the long Minnesota winter. As we unload the car, Linda tilts her head in their direction and says, "All I can think of when I see that is skin cancer and wrinkles."

At the Beach

There is nothing to distinguish our motel room, and it is perfect. It is perfect in its anonymity, its utilitarian modesty. There are two double beds facing a color TV mounted on the wall above the imitation-wood dresser. The mirror over the dresser is big enough to see all of yourself. A heavy double drape covers the picture window. No light comes through and it is absolutely dark in the room when the lights are off. The air conditioner maintains a steady white noise. And this is what we like, Linda and I, the dark motel room, the cool whir of the air conditioner, the locked door, a good shower, clean towels every day, no one who knows us. This is our idea of a perfect vacation.

We change into our suits. Before we fix our straps, we rub suntan lotion on each other's shoulders and backs. My sister's back is pitted from acne. I watch her as she peers into the bright mirror over the dresser to rub suntan lotion on her face, and I see her again at fifteen, leaning over the bathroom sink, chewing her bottom lip. By then she had developed a brooding expression, as if she were contemplating a mystery too deep for her mind to encompass. I lay on my stomach on the hall rug and watched her from the far away safety of childhood, where all skin is clear. She squeezed a pimple and I laughed.

"You think you're so smart!" she said to me with hatred ringing in her voice. "You just wait! Your time will come!"

Then she ran, leaping over me, though I tried to catch her bare ankles, to her yellow room and slammed the door. I imagine she lay on her brown-and-yellow bedspread which matched her brown-and-yellow curtains, and cried.

But she was wrong. My time didn't come. I never developed acne. I didn't make the weekly trips to the dermatologist's, just as I didn't make the weekly trips to the doctor's for allergy shots. I was not allergic to cats, feather pillows, dust, chocolate, citrus, or seafood. I never missed school because of asthma, and I never went to the hospital believing I would die. I took my luck for granted. I was used to being the lucky one.

We walk across the street to the beach, and stand for a moment at the first sight of the ocean. It is stretched out in either direction as far as the eye can see, and deep unto the horizon. It is magnificent. When I touch my bare foot down into the warm sand, it immediately conforms in its gentle heat to my arch. Here the wind blows everything away that is not important enough to be held down. There are people, floats, umbrellas, and the dazzling sun. We catch hold of each other's towels to put them down straight, tugging them back from the wind. We sit on the towels and the sand beneath shapes to our bottoms. Soon my skin seems to relax, as if it had been holding itself tight all winter, and can now let go.

"Remember that time we were in the ocean and something bit you," Linda says, but not really to me. She is sitting on her towel beside me, looking out at the water. "You yelled, 'It's got me and it's big.'" She laughs and I laugh too. I don't remember saying the words. But it sounds like me. I do remember a certain distrust I have always had for the water, for what lives beneath the surface and cannot be seen.

In our struggle to distinguish ourselves one from the other when we were growing up, Linda claimed the water. At the state park where we spent the summers, she became the first girl lifeguard in a time when there were no girl lifeguards. To get her Water Safety Instructor certificate, she had to swim to the dam. I sat on the beach and watched her start out into the shallow water, then go beyond the first ropes, swimming the Australian crawl as smoothly and rhythmically as if she could go forever. Then past the far ropes which kept the row boats out of the swimming area, out into the wide green expanse of the lake and on and on, the lifeguard boat paddling steadily beside her, her head a small bobbing ball as on and on she swam, past the halfway mark, on and on until she disappeared from sight around the bend before the dam. I sat on the sand in my damp suit until I got a chill and then I walked home. The sight of the empty green lake stretching before me had made me feel alone, and a little frightened.

I did not get a WSI. I couldn't even pass the junior lifesaving course. I learned all the strokes, and how to save drowning people, but I was not a believer. I knew that if I tried to save someone who was drowning, he'd use me as a ladder to climb back up into light and air.

I failed finally because I couldn't pass the test of pulling a concrete block off the bottom of the lake. The instructor would throw it off the diving platform, and it would unravel a rope behind it at an alarming rate. The idea was to retrieve it as if it were a body. Almost as soon as my head was underwater, my feet kicking in the air in a futile attempt to propel me downward, I would bob back up to the surface. The water around the diving board was deep and had a strange green light to it below when I opened my eyes to try to find the concrete block. I'd pop back to the surface. I could not make myself go deep.

We are lying on our beds in the motel room. The heavy drapes are pulled. As soon as we shut the door, the whole outside world of heat and light and noise disappeared. Inside it is cool and quiet and dark.

We have been out in the sun all day. Now we have taken showers and smoothed on Jergens lotion, and our sunburned bodies are naked under our summer robes. Linda has fixed us tall glasses of tonic and lime over ice, which are sweating onto the imitation-wood table between our beds.

We are talking about our childhoods, which we always do when we are together. Sometimes we tell the same old stories—the time Linda kicked out my two front baby teeth when we were playing bucking bronco (her) and cowboy (me) at our grandmother's in Texas, and how she hunted for them in the grass so I could put them under my pillow, or about the time Lady got hit by a car, and our boxer dog Blaze came running up to us in the backyard and barked and barked until we went out to the street and found her. It seems we talk more now that we are older, now that we live so far apart and have so little time together. It seems we remember more and more.

"Remember how I had to go to cotillions on Saturday nights," Linda is saying. "Every Saturday night I'd cry and cry, and Mother would make me go. I hadn't matured enough. I should have been outside playing instead of standing around waiting for some pimply faced boy to ask me to dance. Mama could have protected me from that. But no, she forced me to go, week in and week out."

This is a long standing grudge of Linda's, territory we've covered many times before.

"She wanted us to have a social life," I say.

"I'll never forgive her for that," Linda says. "She knew

how miserable it made me."

Sometimes when we talk about our parents, it is as if we're discussing different people. The parents Linda had when she was growing up do not seem to be the same parents I had.

"I'll never forget that time they drove me to college," she says. "I was so nervous and insecure about meeting all those new girls. I had fixed my hair in a flip,"—she demonstrates with a wave of her small hand—"you remember that style, and when we got down there, Mama said, 'Nobody else has her hair fixed like you do.' That just crushed me."

She was always so sensitive. Everything seemed to hurt her—an unkind word, a hard look. "Everything was such a big deal to you," I say.

"Or that time Daddy forgot his camera at my graduation. I mean, you can't come out of the bathroom at our house without having your picture taken, you know? Then he forgot his camera. There isn't a single picture of my graduation."

"He just forgot his camera."

"I bet he didn't forget for yours."

"I didn't go through graduation. I had them mail my diploma."

She has no reply to this.

"We always were so different," I say. Perhaps it was because I was three years younger than Linda. I could watch her mistakes and learn from them.

"I remember one time we got spanked," she says. "We had been jumping on our beds, laughing and carrying on, asking for it you might say, and finally we got it. Only you didn't cry! God did that hurt! I cried so hard and you didn't even cry."

I remember it was a summer night. The window was open and the curtain was blowing into the room. We both had on our nightgowns and mine billowed in the breeze. I was determined not to cry. After that, it didn't even hurt that much.

When I look at Linda, she is not looking at me. She is chewing her lip, and her face has that familiar brooding expression.

Then she sits up. "Don't you feel guilty when you don't send presents on Mother's or Father's Day?" she asks. "That just amazes me. I always send something. I would feel so guilty if I didn't."

It's true that I'm not very sentimental about occasions. I don't always send gifts. Christmas, of course, but I may skip a birthday.

"Well, I figure after thirty-odd years, if they don't know I love them, a present on Mother's Day isn't going to make any difference."

Linda stares at me. "But don't they make you feel guilty? They make me feel so guilty."

I shake my head. "To tell the truth, I've never given it much thought."

We regard each other across the abyss between our two beds. We shake our heads, and laugh a little.

Linda gets up and walks into the bathroom. She doesn't bother to shut the door while she goes.

"What was I like?" I call to her. "When we were growing up."

"Oh, I don't know," she says when she comes back. She gets more tonic from the small refrigerator built into the dresser. She pours us both more tonic and sets the bottle on the rug between the beds, and lies back on her two pillows.

"I don't remember you talking much. You kept to yourself. You'd come home from school and go up to your room and study and read. I hated to do homework. I'd work for ten minutes and then I'd want to watch TV. It wasn't until I went to graduate school that I found out I was smart."

"I don't remember being studious like that," I say, surprised.

"You seemed so detached. Almost like you were hypnotized."

We both think this over in silence.

"One thing I've always felt bad about," I say after awhile. "How I used to jump out and scare you and poke you in your breasts. I must have been about ten. You were just developing."

"I don't remember that," she says, and looks over at me and laughs as if I'd told something funny.

I sit up, unable to believe she can't remember. I've been ashamed of it for years. She was such an easy target. I'd hide around corners and doors and jump out. She always fell for it. For awhile she was a nervous wreck over it.

"I do remember you were mean to me," she says. "You were so little and frail—not sickly—I guess I was the sickly one. But just small, such tiny bones. Everyone thought you were a little china doll. Mama and Daddy used to say to me, don't hurt your little sister! And I was the one getting beat up! I have the scars to prove it." Her voice leaps at the injustice of this.

Then she says in a smaller voice, "I really do think they loved you best."

In the morning, while Linda sleeps, I get up and dress quietly in the total dark, and go out just as the sun is coming up, a big red disk over the ocean. The day is quivering, I can feel the heat waiting in the wings. Other people are out, joggers, people with dogs, a few solitary walkers like myself. When the beach fills up later, it is the human parade. But now there are only a few of us, and I walk at the edge of the water, where the waves come and go, making the sand dark and light before me. Sandpipers run a few paces ahead and in the shallows a school of minnows turns as one.

Occasionally I come upon a sea creature washed ashore, a jellyfish, a crab shell, a broken sand dollar. I hold the piece of sand dollar in my hand. When we were growing up, our parents told us the story of the sand dollar. How the circle in the middle was the crown of thorns and the four dark spots were the holes where they drove the nails, just as we had learned in Sunday school. The dogwood blossom told the same story with its shape of the cross, its bloody stains, and prickly crown. It made the whole world seem connected, as if everything fit together and made sense. I toss the sand dollar back into the waves.

I walk out on one of the long wooden piers that stretch out so far over the ocean. It is a long way to the water, and you can tell it is deep, how it drops off into fathoms. A few solitary fishermen are out, and gulls careen overhead. The sun is getting down to business.

I sit on one of the wooden benches that faces out to sea. It is a high perch, and my feet don't touch down. I look out to sea. No object breaks the great expanse. At the horizon the sea and sky come together like a fold in a piece of paper.

When I get back to our room, Linda is still asleep. I sit on my bed and watch her. Her breathing is deep and steady. Each breath a wave. I sit there for a long time, listening to my sister breathe.

At night we go out to eat, choosing a different seafood restaurant from our parents' list. On our last night, we drive over the North Carolina border to Calabash, which has fifty seafood restaurants and little else. It is the home of the Calabash shrimp, which are tiny and pink and very sweet. In Calabash they fry them in a light batter, and in the restaurant Linda and I sit at one of the bare wood tables, with our silverware wrapped in a paper napkin. They bring us a cold pitcher of ice tea without asking, sweetened with sugar, tart with lemon. We order Captain's Plates to get everything— flounder, deviled crab, oysters, scallops, shrimp, cole slaw, hush puppies.

When we have finished and said over and over, as we always do, that this is the best seafood we have ever had, we go out into the lovely Southern evening.

It is that beautiful time of night at the beach, oyster light. We stroll down to the dock behind the restaurant where the shrimp boats come in. They are selling shrimp to customers by the pound, and there is a salty seacoast smell in the air. Against the bright blue of the water and the bright green of the sea grass, the boats look very grey and weathered.

My sister takes my picture, I take hers. I see her through the camera in her sun dress. I have tied the straps myself on her shoulders, the shape of which I know so well, helping her adjust them, as she has tied mine. They are dresses with elastic across the bodice, one size fits all, and we have bought them at different places at different times but they are the same. We wear them like sisters.

I see my sister through the camera. I will remember this day, this evening at the beach for a long time, forever. I will remember my sister at this moment, not as the photograph will show her, but as I *know* her—what hurts her and what is hard for her, how much I care for her and how worried I am for her, her happiness, her well-being, how little I can affect it, and so I snap the picture and we rush on.

We drive slowly through Calabash and stop at an old house which has been converted into a souvenir shop. It has a big graceful porch, strung now with Pawley Island hammocks. There are all manner of objects to buy—the same ones they sold when we were children, for here at the beach, nothing ever changes, it is always the same.

We wander down the aisles of shells and straw hats, the wooden salad bowls and glass lanterns from Japan. Linda buys a shark-tooth necklace for a new boyfriend, I buy a blue T-shirt for my husband, we buy salt-water taffy for our folks. For myself, I buy a pink-and-white conch shell, the kind you hold to your ear to hear the ocean.

The last day of our vacation, we go out just in the morning. We will drive back this afternoon—four hours to home, and then tomorrow we'll leave for our other homes— Tennessee, Minnesota. We go out on the beach and we rent floats from the teenage lifeguard whose hair is sunbleached, whose tan could be in a Coppertone ad. He is part of what never changes at the beach, and while we have grown older, he has not changed and will be here every year.

The floats are the same, navy blue canvas with rope handles, and we drag them into the surf, and we float on them, rhythmically with the waves, and we sit astride them and ride them to shore. The current carries us far down the beach, and we get out and walk back up the beach, dragging the floats by the rope handles. We plunge into the ocean again, and the waves lift us and carry us in. We try for the big waves, the ones that will carry us all the way in.

Once when I ride a wave in, I stand for a moment on the

beach, and look back to sea. I see my sister on a float in the ocean. She is looking behind her to catch a big wave. She rides the wave and it lifts her up and she shouts like a happy child.

All the Way to East Texas

Miriam Swenson was lying in bed, half awake, half asleep, with her husband Ted when the phone rang. It was an early Monday morning in July, and they were taking a few extra moments to enjoy the cool air, the rain. They had spent the weekend at Rainbo, Ted's grandfather's cabin in northern Wisconsin, and they had gotten in late. They ran over a cat on the way back. Ted was driving, they were going seventy miles per hour. The cat was orange, it crouched down right in the middle of the dark country road, and they zoomed over it. Miriam tensed, expecting to hear some horrible crunch or thump, but there was nothing. When they drove back to see, the cat was watching them from the side of the road, its chartreuse eyes shining. In the car lights, it leaped and ran into the high grass of the shoulder. They hadn't hurt it at all.

Miriam leaped out of bed at the first ring. There was that funny sound, like a vacuum, that alerted her to long distance. And then in a garbled way, she heard that her father had died. It was her mother, crying a little, saying her father had passed away yesterday.

She didn't feel a thing. She carried the phone back into the bedroom and sat on the bed, and told Ted her father had died, and she felt him patting her back. But her mother was saying something about how her grandmother had died, and Miriam thought, they both died? How could they both die? It was very confusing, very garbled. Much like a dream.

Then her mother pulled herself together and explained. It was not her father who had died, it was Grandmother. When she first started talking, she tried to say Miriam's name, to address her, but she had started to cry, and it had come out sounding like Miriam's father's name, William. Miriam had thought she said "William...passed away."

Now tears spurted from Miriam's eyes, because her grandmother was finally dead, but at the same time, she felt relief, it was not as bad as she first thought, it was not her father. And everything seemed all right.

It was so early in the morning, and the news was so sudden that Miriam had trouble understanding certain things. It seemed that her parents were not at home in South Carolina, but were somewhere in Tennessee. They had left yesterday to drive to Texas, where her grandmother was to be buried, and now they were halfway there. They hadn't been able to reach Miriam up north, and besides, there was nothing she could do. Miriam began to see that events were already underway. She'd been out in a boat on a lake in northern Wisconsin, cooking steaks, making love in a king-size bed, while her parents were making arrangements for her grandmother's body to be sent to Texarkana for burial.

And it shocked Miriam that they were driving. Of course

they used to drive to Texarkana every summer when Miriam was growing up, to visit her grandmother—that was before Miriam's mother moved her grandmother to South Carolina, first to a red-brick duplex, and then to the nursing home—but now that they were so old, the idea of her two little parents jockeying for lanes on the super highways with semi-trucks frightened Miriam. It mystified her that they continued to think of themselves as the people they had always been. It had not yet occurred to them that they were old.

As her mother talked, Miriam wondered if she should fly to Texas for the funeral. They'd talked about it for years, knowing her grandmother would one day be buried in Texarkana, and that Miriam would be somewhere far away—Minnesota, as it turned out. At times her mother had said she definitely wanted Miriam to be there, and at other times, other years, she had said it wouldn't be necessary.

"Do you think I should come?" Miriam asked, and her mother was hesitant on the other end. She paused.

"I don't think you need to. It's such a long way from Minneapolis to Texarkana. And we're just going to have a simple graveside service."

"Distance isn't a problem," Miriam said, hesitantly. "Flying, I can be there in a few hours."

"Your father is trying to tell me something," her mother said. Miriam could hear him in the background. She pictured the motel room in Tennessee where they were staying. Her father had always enjoyed the drive to Texas.

"Now Honey," he came on the line, "don't you even think of coming way down here. Mother's getting along just fine. She's doing real well, and you don't need to come all this way."

Her father was so adamant that Miriam didn't argue. She was doing what she always did when someone told her what to do: she bided her time, knowing she'd make up her own mind in the end. It was already taking shape that she would fly to Texas. Not because she should be there. Not because her mother needed her. But because she wanted to. She didn't want to miss it.

When Miriam hung up, she fell back onto the bed, and cried a little, but when Ted got up and went in to shave, she followed him and sat on the closed toilet seat, and talked to him about how she thought it was her father, and how relieved she was it was only her grandmother. "Only Grandmother!" she said, and laughed, feeling uncomfortable. Miriam wanted to have the correct thoughts, the correct feelings, though often she didn't.

Over breakfast they talked about whether she should fly down for the funeral. She had to teach a class on Tuesday, or reschedule it, which was unthinkable to Miriam—calling all those people, having the course run an extra week, and some of the students had vacations planned after the last class. She thought she could teach, and then fly down on Tuesday evening in time for the funeral on Wednesday. They decided to talk about it that evening, when they'd had time to think about it more. And Ted went off to work.

As soon as he was out the door, Miriam was on the phone to the airline. She had posed the question to herself: Do you want to go? And the answer was a surprising, overwhelming *yes*. For one thing, the funeral would be a chance to see her parents. Miriam saw them maybe once a year, which surprised her. She hadn't realized when she was growing up that it would be that way. And she'd get to see her Texas relatives—her great-aunt Annie, her uncle Elmo, her cousins Texana and Joey. Miriam hadn't seen Texana and Joey in years. They were grown now, with children of their own, but when Miriam knew them, they had been the children. She was twelve or thirteen when her grandmother moved to South Carolina, and those hot summer trips to Texas had stopped. Her memories of Texarkana felt like the memories of childhood itself, random but vivid. She wanted to go there again, the way one wants to remember a dream after waking up.

Ted drove her to the airport on Tuesday after her class. Miriam felt strangely elated, as if she were off on a vacation.

"Give your mother my sympathy," Ted said, and grinned. "Even though your grandmother was kind of a pain in the butt."

Miriam had to laugh. It was true her grandmother had gotten to be quite a problem in her old age. Those last years in the nursing home, she had imagined that there were babies in her bed. She was afraid she'd smother them when she fell asleep.

"The funny thing is," Miriam said as they walked through the crowded terminal, "I can't believe how much I'm looking forward to going back there. There were years when I wouldn't have set foot in Texas!"

"Your long-hair hippie days."

He meant the years Miriam lived in California. Those were the war years, when LBJ was a personal affront to everyone she knew. If anyone mistook her accent for a Texas one, she'd quickly let him know she was from South Carolina. Bad, but not as bad as Texas.

Miriam caught a commuter flight from Dallas to Texarkana on an airline she had never heard of, Rio. There were eight or nine businessmen on board. Several of them wore boots. They sat in single file on either side of the tiny plane in seats that seemed made for children. There was no partition between the passengers and pilots. Miriam noticed the co-pilot was a lot younger than she. It was dark in the plane except for the lights on the flight panel. There was a lot of noise and vibration, and no one said a word the whole way.

Her parents and her uncle Elmo met her at the airport in Texarkana. They looked as if they were from the same tribe. Miriam wondered if anyone would be able to tell she belonged to them. Her father had on bright red pants, and a red-and-white-striped polo shirt. He had a white belt around his girth, and imitation-lizard white shoes. Miriam laughed when she saw that outfit. Her uncle Elmo had on the same kind of clothes, only his pants were dark blue, his polo shirt, light blue. Her mother had on a bright red dress and Keds. "You and Daddy are color-coordinated," Miriam said to her.

"I don't know how that happened!" her mother said and laughed, grabbing hold of Miriam's arm. "I almost didn't know who that was getting off that plane."

"I didn't have any trouble recognizing you!"

Her father insisted on carrying her duffle bag. She hadn't checked any luggage through.

"Did you bring something to wear to the funeral?" her mother said, looking at the bag.

"I've got it on," Miriam said. She was wearing her one good summer suit, a beige linen.

"You've got it on?" Uncle Elmo said. Miriam had forgotten her uncle's habit of repeating what any of the women and children said, as if it were the most asinine thing he had ever heard. If one of them made a simple request, such as "pass the sugar," he'd pass it, but not before repeating in a querulous voice, "pass the sugar?" It had been a constant, predictable echo on those summer visits.

"Sure wish Ted could have come," her father said jovially, rhetorically. Miriam could not imagine him here. He belonged to her future, not to her past.

"When did you'all get into Texarkana?" Miriam asked when they got in the car.

"Oh we made great time," her father said. "I know the way like the back of my hand."

"I don't let your daddy drive after dark," her mother said, sitting beside Miriam in the backseat.

"Don't let him drive after dark?" Uncle Elmo said.

"You'all should have flown," Miriam said. "It would have been so much easier."

"Oh we didn't want to pack to fly," her mother said.

That night her mother sat in her slip on one of the twin beds in the room where Miriam was staying—her cousin Joey's old room, which still smelled, it seemed to Miriam, of model airplane glue—and told Miriam the story of her mother's death. She and Miriam's father were over at the lake when they got the call from the nursing home that her mother's pulse was weakening, her breath fading.

"And do you know that by the time we got there, she was gone! They had already packed up all her things in big plastic bags. The only things left in that room were the TV set and her."

Miriam didn't know what to say. "That fast!"

"Oh they have a waiting list a mile long," her mother continued, animated and full of facts. "And to tell the truth, I'm just as glad. It saved us having to do it. Those nurses have been so good to us. I'll have to take them a box of candy or something when I get back."

Her mother seemed a little breathless.

"How are you doing, Mother?"

"Oh, I'm sure I'll feel it when all this is over," her mother said, sweeping her hand to indicate the room, and by extension, Miriam guessed, the trip to Texas for the funeral. "You expect it for so long, and then when it finally happens, it takes you by surprise." She gave Miriam a quizzical look. "I was just over there on Friday, and she was fine."

Miriam had trouble getting to sleep that night. The central air-conditioning kept going on and off, and it seemed timed to her own rhythms, silent until the very moment when she was about to drop off, then jerking on in a way that jolted her awake. Oddly, perhaps because she was in Texas— instead of her grandmother's death, she thought of the death of John Kennedy. Miriam had been in high school when Kennedy was killed. The librarian at her school was named Kennedy, and at first Miriam thought that it was he who had been shot. After she understood, she went outside and looked up into the sky. She had expected the Russians to fly over and drop bombs.

Her great-aunt Annie came over the next morning after breakfast. She was driving a '63 Buick, with 27,000 miles on it. "How's my little girl?" she cried, embracing Miriam in a big strong hug. Her hair was already pure white when

Miriam was a child, and she looked exactly as she had then, even to the black mole, like a beauty mark, on her beautiful rouged cheek.

Miriam drove her parents, her uncle, and Annie to the funeral home. On the way through town, her mother, who had grown up in Texarkana, pointed out the landmarks. Miriam didn't remember Texarkana being so small and run-down. When they crossed State Line, she thought of how she and Linda used to try to impress their friends back home with the fact that in Texarkana, you could stand with one foot in Texas and one in Arkansas. They passed several Western stores. Miriam and Linda had always wanted to stop. They had wanted gun-and-holster sets, tooled belts, pointy-toed boots, Indian stuff.

In the viewing room, her grandmother was laid out in a shiny white coffin lined with pink velvet, like a doll in a box. She looked diminished, with an absence of color. Her hands—the skin so sheer it revealed bone and vein underneath—were folded on her chest. Someone had dressed her in her blue pants suit with the polka-dot tie.

Her mother and Uncle Elmo only stayed a moment. Miriam's mother was as diligent in death as she had been in life to take care of her mother's business. She wanted to make sure the flowers got delivered to the grave site in time for the service. Miriam's father leaned over the casket, peering through his bifocals, and said to no one in particular, "I think she looks real good."

Her great-aunt took Miriam's hand. Being with her made Miriam feel about seven again. "How do you like the casket?" she asked. The casket had a bright enamel surface like a tooth, with a lot of brass fixtures. Miriam wasn't sure what her tastes were in caskets.

"I know she would have liked it," Annie said. "Your mother and I picked it out yesterday."

"It's very nice."

They stood there awhile longer. Her great-aunt did not let go of Miriam's hand. Miriam was thinking with relief that she did not feel too sad. Her grandmother's death was not, after all, a heart-rending thing. But even as she was thinking those thoughts—emotion—as if it had a life of its own—welled up in her, and she found that she was crying. Beside her, her great-aunt wiped her eyes with a white handkerchief. Then Miriam's feeling, on its own, subsided. She noticed that her grandmother's gold wedding ring was missing. She had secretly coveted that ring. She used to stare at it in the nursing home, fascinated by how the years had worn the gold so thin.

At the graveside service, they sat in metal chairs under the canopy the funeral home had erected to provide some shade. The indoor-outdoor carpeting was bunched somehow. Miriam's chair was unstable. Once, at the risk of toppling over, she turned to look for her cousins Texana and Joey in the knot of people crowding behind them to get out of the Texas sun, but she wasn't able to spot them. The service was scheduled for early in the day, but already heat waves were shimmering across the cemetery.

The preacher took his place in front of them, almost near enough to touch. In his brown leisure suit and blow-dried hair, he reminded Miriam of a game-show host. He spoke to the family informally, with a certain intimacy, as if he'd known them all his life. The cadences of his East Texas accent wafted over them in the July heat, kindly and sincere. Though Miriam was no longer a believer, she listened to the old-time religion with the same dreamy attention she gave to fairy tales as a child. The preacher spoke of bodily resurrection. They could all expect to see their loved one again in the flesh. Life after death. Behind them she heard the soft swoosh of fans.

Beside her her father shook his foot a little, perhaps to stay awake. Miriam could tell that his mind floated free. She had always liked to be near her father for moments such as this. She had many memories of driving deep into the South Carolina foothills with her father to visit the country relatives. The men would sit on the porch and rock, to just *be*.

A sob broke free, rose independently into the bright sleepy air, like a red balloon of sound someone had released. At first Miriam thought it was her mother. Everyone shifted in the precarious chairs. Out of the corner of her eye, Miriam saw her great-aunt's face, working. Then she realized it was her uncle Elmo. She had never thought of Uncle Elmo as someone who would sob.

She had been afraid of him as a child. All the other adults in her life were kind and gentle. It had confused her that he could be the way he was, and that everyone went right on, behaving towards him as they did towards everyone else. It didn't seem right.

Her aunt Dora had called him Ellie—a pet name. "Oh pipe down, Ellie," she'd say, as if he weren't so bad. She had died several years ago, of leukemia. She had had straight black hair with bangs and a face round as a plate. Maybe she was part Mexican, though no one ever said so. She liked hot Mexican food, and made a dirty joke about having to sit in the creek the next day. In another of those random, vivid memories Miriam had of Texas, she remembered that Aunt Dora had made the first cheesecake she ever had. She had thought something called cheesecake would be awful, until she tasted it.

The preacher had come to the part where he was recounting Miriam's grandmother's life. He described how she married at sixteen, and moved to Texarkana from Marietta, South Carolina. She had three children, one of whom gave his life for the country. That was Miriam's uncle Johnny, killed at age twenty-three in the Second World War. There was a time in Miriam's life, when, looking at the photograph of Uncle Johnny—that smiling young man in a uniform—she could not imagine reaching the age of twenty-three herself. Now that she was in her thirties, she understood better why it used to make the women leave the room in tears just to hear Johnny's name.

"I want you to meet Roy," Texana said. She and Miriam had hugged lightly, and now she had stepped back. Despite the fact that her high heels were sinking into the soft earth near the grave, she was still taller than her husband Roy. She was beautiful in the way Miriam thought beautiful was supposed to be years ago—Miss America-style. Miriam wondered if there was something about Texas—in the air or water maybe—that made for very tall girls with high cheekbones and dazzling smiles. Texas smiles, she thought of them.

Roy grabbed Miriam's hand and gave it a good shake. He had on what Miriam took to be his funeral face. His brown hound-dog eyes were so earnest it made Miriam want to laugh out loud. She could tell he wouldn't be able to hold that face for long.

Miriam had been curious to meet this newest husband. She hadn't met either of Texana's first two husbands. The first time she got married, Miriam's parents flew out to Texas for the wedding. There were pictures of Texana, statuesque and smiling, in her long white dress. Within a year or two, she had a daughter, and then they got the bad news: Texana was getting a divorce. Miriam's parents had been shocked. But perhaps because Miriam was living in California then, divorce didn't surprise her. It seemed, if anything, predictable.

Not long after Texana's divorce, Miriam's sister Linda got divorced. Miriam's mother had to tell her own bad news to the Texas relatives. Then Texana got married again. Another daughter, another divorce. By the time she got married a third time, to Roy, no one told Miriam's parents. They found out when Annie slipped up on the phone, and let the latest cat out of the bag.

Miriam was thirty-three when she finally married, for the first and so far only time. She had spent her twenties on a number of love affairs, a few of which were disastrous. Once Ted accused her of being afraid of marriage. Miriam had corrected him. It was divorce she was afraid of.

At the funeral dinner, Texana sat on a footstool at Roy's feet, her arm draped across his lap. She looked as if she might lay her head there. When they were children, Texana had wanted to be a Rangette. She and Miriam and Linda had practiced cheers in the backyard of their grandmother's house, under the pecan trees. Texana had been pudgy as a child, but she had grown into a tall long-legged beauty. She looked like a Rangette, but she had become a physical therapist.

Her cousin Joey and his wife Lorraine, another tall Texas girl, sat on the couch, holding a bald baby who looked around at everybody with a bewildered expression. Joey had been the baby of the four cousins. He had grinned all the time, as if something invisible were constantly tickling him. Now he looked like a Dallas Cowboy, grinning. He had a job as a well watcher. According to Uncle Elmo, Joe sometimes had to watch oil wells for eighteen hours at a stretch. According to Uncle Elmo, it was a good job to have in Texas.

Miriam thought there might be some anecdotes about her grandmother that she had never heard. But no one mentioned her. Instead, Roy was just waiting for an opening to introduce the topic of fishing, and once he found it, they all sat back and watched.

Once he asked Miriam what kind of fish they caught in Minnesota, but as she was about to answer, he launched into a new story about the time he caught a shark off the pier at Galveston, and how they had to shoot it with a .38 to kill it.

"We have two boats," Texana said as they sat around eating the food the church women had brought over off paper plates, and drinking big glasses of iced tea. "One small one and one big enough for all of us. Roy has two children too from a previous marriage." She had the exact same smile she had had as a child, and her voice sounded exactly as Miriam remembered it. She even answered Miriam's parents as she did as a child, "Yes, Ma'am," and "No, Sir."

"That one there," Roy said, pointing his fork at Lorraine. "That one there can eat her weight in catfish. Whoooeeeee! That gal'll eat you under the table!"

When Lorraine laughed, the deepest dimples Miriam had ever seen formed in her cheeks.

"How do you like all this fishing?" Miriam's mother

asked Texana in a voice that told Miriam what her mother thought of it.

"Oh I like it fine now," Texana drawled. "Just sittin' in the back of the boat, no phone to answer, nothing to do. Roy says I like fishing so much now he never gets to go by himself anymore." She laughed as she said this. They all laughed.

"Never gets to go by hisself anymore?" Uncle Elmo began, but Roy was already talking, rearing back on the tips of Aunt Dora's antique chair, his pants legs riding up his cowboy boots.

"She caught the prize!" he shouted. "Texana, she sure did!" His face was going in all directions, as if he could barely contain himself. "She sure did, a fourteen-inch striper bass."

"We're having it mounted," Texana said modestly.

"She may have caught the prize," Roy said. "But I was the coach! I was the coach!"

After dinner they drove by Miriam's grandmother's old house in a little caravan. Miriam drove her parents in their car, and Uncle Elmo drove Annie in hers. Up ahead were Roy and Texana in a big white sedan, and ahead of them, Joey and Lorraine and the baby in a pickup truck with a gun rack.

When Miriam's grandmother moved to South Carolina, they sold the old place on Pine Street, and it was turned into rental property. It looked very run-down, and had been painted, of all things, pink. Miriam's mother asked her to drive through the alley behind so she could see the pecan trees. Miriam remembered how her grandmother used to throw the bath water out onto the St. Augustine grass to save it during summer droughts. She saw the fire escape that led up to Miss Steven's apartment. Miss Steven was her grandmother's boarder. A string of chimes from India had hung on her door. They made a little ripple of sound when she opened the door.

Miriam had made her reservations back for Sunday, which left three days to get through at Uncle Elmo's. She didn't know why she had wanted to stay so long. She hadn't even thought to bring a book along, and it was too hot to go outside. She spent her time looking through *Reader's Digest* and *Prevention* magazines while she waited to drive the old folks to the cafeteria or a fast-food restaurant for the next meal.

One afternoon she was lying on one of the twin beds in Joey's room, reading a story about a man whose mother had been tortured and killed in Greece during the war. The air conditioner was going on and off, and she heard, intermittently, the voices of her mother and great-aunt in the den. Her father and Uncle Elmo had gone to the farmer's market, and her mother and Annie were taking their afternoon rest. Her mother was stretched out in the La-Z-Boy rocker, her great-aunt on the Naugahyde couch. As she read on, in a torpor of boredom, with one part of her mind she played with the idea of flying back to Minneapolis early. She could go in and tell her mother and Annie that she had decided to fly back that day. They'd be surprised, and maybe even hurt, but they'd have to understand. She thought of other people she knew, and she couldn't imagine anyone being in her position. It seemed weird to be thirty-six years old, lying on a twin bed in East Texas, reading a *Reader's Digest.*

But still she read on, compelled, in a way, to find out if the narrator avenged his mother's death, as he so wanted to do. Then she heard what she thought was crying. She sat up and listened, but the air conditioner came back on. When it went off again, Miriam realized that it was her mother who was crying. Her great-aunt was comforting her. Their words didn't make much sense. They came to Miriam disjointed, elliptical. "You have to go on with your own life now," she heard her great-aunt murmur.

Miriam felt lightheaded, as if she might float. Maybe she should go to her mother. But then she realized that what her mother needed right now was mothering, which was something that Miriam, as her child, could not give her.

At the funeral Miriam's mother had made a big point to Texana about getting to see her children before they left. But by Saturday afternoon, they still hadn't heard from her.

"How do I know when she's going to bring the girls over?" Uncle Elmo said, in response to Miriam's mother's latest inquiry on the subject. But he went to the phone to find out.

"Not home?" they heard him say. "Well, have her give me a call when she comes in."

"That was one of the kids," he said to them when he hung up. "I guess she's out running around somewhere."

Miriam saw her mother and great-aunt exchange female looks of worry. It did seem odd that they hadn't seen more of Texana.

By that evening, they still hadn't heard from her.

"She must not have gotten the message," Annie ventured. "Why don't you call her again, Elmo?"

"Call her again?" But he went to the phone and dialed. This time Roy must have answered, for they heard Uncle Elmo ask when Texana was going to bring the girls over for the South Carolina relatives to see.

"Getting a divorce!" they heard him exclaim.

Miriam glanced at her mother and Annie. They looked as if they had received word of another death. But Miriam, sitting in the La-Z-Boy rocker, couldn't help but find something darkly funny in that familiar echo.

On Sunday morning, Texana came over with her two girls.

"I wanted you'all to see them before you left," she said. She looked tired, with dark circles under her eyes, like a beauty queen the day after the pageant.

At first the girls were shy, but soon they got over that. Miriam couldn't help staring at them. She was fascinated by the intangible Texana-like quality they each had. Amy, seven, was tall and sinewy, proud that she could read. Penny, four, was barely over being a baby. She looked up at Miriam like a kitten.

They wanted Miriam to see their sister routines. Texana and Miriam went with them into the backyard, and stood under the big trees which had been little trees the last time Miriam was in Texas. Amy showed her the cheers she knew, yelling "fight, fight, fight" in her flat Texas accent, swiveling her hips, twirling her arms, going down on one knee, leaping into the air. Penny tried to do the cheers too, though she forgot the words and got her arms so mixed up she fell on the grass in a giggling heap.

Then another of those random, vivid memories came to

Miriam. "Do you remember how we used to play Big Cats?" she asked Texana.

Texana looked at her and laughed, and shook her head, no.

"Oh," Miriam said, laughing herself, "we'd get down on all fours, arch our backs, rub up against things. Purr." She shook her head, to think of it. Texana had made such a wonderful cat. Miriam had actually been able to see the plume of her tail, and the whiskers sprouting from her beautiful feline face.

That afternoon, her parents, Uncle Elmo, and Annie drove Miriam to the airport. On the way, Uncle Elmo told them that Texana had moved out of the house she and Roy rented, and was staying with the girls in the Ramada Inn. She was taking them swimming in the pool that afternoon, as a treat.

At the airport Miriam told them not to park and come in. Her parents were starting the drive back to South Carolina, and she wanted them to get a good start. She said her good-byes in the air-conditioned car. But her father got out anyway. "You don't have to come in," she said to him. "They're all waiting."

"Oh let 'em wait," her father said, dismissing the others with a wave of his hand. He carried Miriam's bag into the terminal, and they stood together at the picture window, and watched a plane take off.

Feeding the Eagles

"How can we buy a cabin in South Carolina when we live in Minnesota, and can't even afford our own house yet?" Ted says to Miriam. He is leaning against the little five-horsepower motor in the back of the Alumacraft boat, wearing a red flannel shirt and canvas fishing cap.

Miriam, sitting in the other end of the boat, doesn't bother to answer. It's a rhetorical question anyway, but then so was hers. She wasn't serious when she suggested they buy her parents' cabin. It was more an expression of her feelings. She stares at the bank of birch on the shore.

"You have a new cabin to come to now," Ted tries again.

Miriam gives him a look that says 'you can't possibly understand.' She knows this is not only unfair but untrue.

Several years ago, when Miriam's father's business failed, her parents had to sell their house. But at least they were able to hold onto the cabin. Now it has become clear that they really cannot afford to keep it up anymore, and besides, they have grown old. Neither Miriam nor her sister Linda will ever live in South Carolina again. It doesn't make sense—even to Miriam—to hang on to it.

"It's just that being at Rainbo makes me think about the cabin," Miriam says. Rainbo is Ted's grandfather's cottage in northern Wisconsin, where they're spending this summer weekend. It's a classic North Woods place, massive logs painted tan with white trim, a porch of windows that crank open to the lake, old wicker furniture, high ceilings of hand-hewn beams, an enormous stone fireplace. And while Rainbo is as different from her cabin as northern Wisconsin is from South Carolina, being here does make Miriam think of it, especially now that she is about to lose it.

When they were first married and had just moved to Minnesota, Ted couldn't wait to bring her to Rainbo. In Washington State, where they lived together while Ted was in law school, Miriam had searched out many cabins for them to go to—one at the foot of Mt. Rainier, another overlooking the Pacific at Kalaloch, another on San Juan Island. "It's a good thing you married somebody with a good cabin," Ted had kidded her on their wedding day.

That first visit, Miriam stood on the grass and admired Rainbo. It was situated on a little rise between two lakes, almost surrounded by water. Inside, it had the same knotty-pine walls, of deep gold, like clover honey, as her cabin. There were old *New Yorker* cartoons and yellowing French menus on the walls, and snapshots of unidentifiable men holding up huge catches of fish.

Though Miriam had admired Rainbo immediately, she had held her feelings a little in abeyance. She wasn't about to commit herself so readily to this Johnny-come-lately cabin.

"Don't you want to talk about it?" Ted asks now, about her own cabin, but Miriam shakes her head, no. The pending loss of her cabin seems so solely her problem, her sorrow, she doesn't want to share it. She looks across at Ted at the other end of the boat, and at the moment, the distance seems insurmountable. She can't imagine crawling across the middle seat, taking a place beside him, laying her head on his shoulder. It strikes her how strange it is that they are married—two people who have been strangers for most of their lives. How strange it is, she thinks, that two strangers should try to become family to one another.

And besides, why spoil his day? He's happy in the little boat on the little lake. In his red flannel shirt and canvas fishing cap, he even looks the part of the North Woods fisherman. Maybe it is actually in his blood.

That first time they came to Rainbo, in keeping with what she figured was the spirit of the place, Miriam had tried fishing. As soon as her Dardevle hit the water, she caught a muskie. People come from all over the world to the North Woods to try to catch a muskie! Ted told her. He took her picture holding the muskie up back at the dock. In the photograph, the muscle of her arm was roped from the effort of hoisting it aloft.

Though Miriam was smiling in the picture (she thought she was supposed to), she was actually feeling sick. Catching the muskie had made her lose whatever initial interest she might have had in fishing. Ted had had to hold the muskie down with his foot in the bottom of the boat, and wrench the hook out. The muskie had taken it deep. It squeaked and thrashed about in the bottom of the boat, with Ted's big rubber boot trying to hold it still. Even Ted got enough of fishing that day.

Now when they go out, Miriam doesn't fish. She usually brings a book along, or her journal, or she just watches for

wildlife. Today they've seen two deer, a loon, and a por-
cupine, which they followed in the boat as he scrambled
along on the shore. But now Miriam just looks down into
the dark clear water. She tries to send messages to the fish,
warning them not to bite.

That evening Miriam sits with her feet on the ledge of the
Franklin stove on the porch. Even though it is summer, they
are far enough north to need a fire. Later they'll sleep in the
big bed under a down quilt.

Ted is lying on the couch reading *Rabbit is Rich*. Every
now and then he laughs out loud. Once he reads Miriam a
funny scene in which Rabbit's wife falls asleep while they're
making love. When Miriam read the book, she hadn't seen
that the scene was comic. Now she laughs too. She catches a
phrase she likes, "importunate flesh."

Miriam is reading her old journal from the year they met,
in a non-credit creative writing class at San Francisco State.
Ted was staying with friends that spring, waiting to hear if
he had been accepted to law school. Miriam had finished
graduate school at Berkeley, and had moved across the Bay.
The first thing they had in common was that they were not
from California.

"Texas?" Ted had asked the first time they talked, during
a break in the three-hour evening class. They were standing
beside a coffee machine that released the coffee and cream
before the cup.

"South Carolina," Miriam drawled. "How 'bout you?"

"Minnesota," Ted said. "Home of lutefisk and lefse."

Miriam had never heard of those things. She had heard of
Minnesota, but only barely.

To explain why he wanted to go to law school in

Washington State, Ted said it had always seemed symmetrical to him to go East to college and West to law school, and besides, he had scored low on his LSAT's—"next to monkey," he had put it, making Miriam laugh, for the first of many times. She had been pleased to discover in herself this laughing woman.

At the end of the summer, when Ted moved to Washington State, Miriam went with him. She got a job in the university's public relations office, and by the time Ted finished law school, the point of living together had escaped her, and she, who had never expected to marry, let alone happily, married Ted and was happy and followed him like a bride back to his hometown.

She is up to Christmas of their first year together. She reads how Ted got a D- on his Civil Procedure test. It was an advisory, a mid-year test that didn't count. "My world stopped," Miriam reads, and laughs uncomfortably to herself, embarrassed to see that she could write such a phrase.

"I'm to the part about your advisories," she says. "Remember those?"

"Sure," Ted says from the couch. "They were advising me to quit."

Miriam laughs, but she doesn't read him the part about the D-, the line, "my world stopped." He knows that part of the story well enough already.

But now Ted is a lawyer, and Miriam is still trying to be a writer. They're alike in that they worry that they're not too good at what they do. Law and writing are both hard professions.

That night before she goes to bed, Miriam writes in the journal she keeps now. She describes the summer day, the boat on the lake, Ted in his red shirt, the conversation in which she asked him if they could buy the cabin. It is an old habit, this business of writing things down.

Miriam has year after year of journals. She keeps all her old papers. She has a filing cabinet full of files on her old boyfriends and her women friends. There are files for her parents, and her sister, in which she puts their letters and the photographs they send. There is even a file on the cabin, with snapshots, a paper place mat from the lodge, and a few dried leaves glued to construction paper, identified in her fourteen-year-old handwriting. Miriam is the kind of person who does not like to let go.

By January, Minnesota is frozen solid. Her parents have not yet sold the cabin. Over long distance, they tell Miriam all about the economy, how people don't have any money, and besides, they haven't tried too hard. Now that it's winter, no one buys a summer place. They'll put it on the market again in the spring. Miriam decides to fly home, visit her folks, and see the cabin again before it is sold.

After a few hours, a few days at home, Miriam will get over the first moment of seeing her parents. But that first moment—when she walks from the plane across the windy expanse of the runway to her hometown's miniature terminal—that first moment, when she sees them pressed against the guard rail, their eager tiny faces searching for hers—that moment is hard on Miriam. She is always shocked to see that they have grown old. Her father's hair is white, and her mother has shrunk, and takes her arm like an old woman when they walk to the baggage claim. Her father insists on carrying her bag, and it seems almost to topple him when he lifts it off the conveyor belt.

But it has been this way for several years now (their age,

her shock)—and in a few hours, a few days, it wears off, and they are to Miriam as they have always been.

One night she takes them out to eat. There is a fancy new steak-and-seafood restaurant in town, but it is too dark for her father, who likes a lot of light on his food. The hostess is wearing the kind of dress Miriam used to wear to high school dances. She seats them near the swinging doors of the kitchen, which was not what Miriam had in mind, but at least her father can see his meal.

Her parents have dressed up for this occasion. Before they left the house, her father stood in the den, and holding onto the TV set for balance, rubbed first one shoe and then the other on the back of his pants legs. He had Miriam's mother fix his hair, stooping down so she could comb it in back.

Her mother is wearing her fiftieth-wedding-anniversary dress, from two years ago. She made a joke about this dress then, saying what her own mother, Miriam's grandmother Homer, said about every new dress she got for the last ten years: "Well, you can bury me in this dress." Miriam and her mother always laughed about it, but it wasn't so funny to Miriam when her mother said it about her own dress.

Miriam had asked her parents on the occasion of their golden anniversary a lot of questions about their wedding and honeymoon, but of course she did not get all the answers she wanted. Her mother remembered exactly what she wore, and her father told how her whole trousseau had been stolen from the running board of the Ford, where they had roped the suitcases for the honeymoon to Hot Springs, Arkansas, but what Miriam wanted to know was *how does it feel to be married for fifty years? How did you manage to become family to each other?*

Now her parents order vodka and tonics, which come in

huge goblets. They drink them from tiny cocktail straws, their little faces dipping over those big drinks. The conversation turns to weather. Last night when Ted called Miriam, he told her a big blizzard had passed through Minnesota, leaving a foot of snow. Miriam's father is interested in the weather in Minnesota. He watches the evening news to see what it is "doing" up there. Miriam is grateful that Minnesota has so much weather. She's grateful that the same sky above stretches from Minnesota to South Carolina. Weather is something they'll always have in common.

Their steaks come, her parents' well done, hers rare. Her mother recalls all the good steaks they used to barbecue at Table Rock. They've talked about the cabin a little since Miriam has been home, and she's been surprised to realize her parents aren't all that sad about selling it. In fact, they're somewhat anxious that they won't be able to find a buyer.

"We've left just about everything up there," her father tells her now, shaking too much salt on his steak. "We're selling it with all the furniture, as is."

"Unless you and Ted want some of the things," her mother adds.

It takes Miriam a moment to absorb this new information. She hadn't thought to ask what would become of the things in the cabin. But, of course, it makes sense to sell it furnished.

"I wanted to hold onto the cabin for you and Linda," her father is saying to her. "But it's just sitting up there in the woods, with no one to look after it."

Miriam nods her head.

"It just takes so much to live on these days," her mother says. "We can't afford to keep it anymore."

"I know," Miriam says. Until a few years ago, she hadn't

realized that such a thing as the cabin would come down to economics. But now she understands how much comes down, simply, to money.

"I was kind of hoping you and Ted could buy it," her father said. "But it would be foolish for you to put money into a place you can't use."

Her father's hands shake a little as they hold his knife and fork in mid-air. They look old, the skin stretched so thin that Miriam sees the large blue veins underneath.

"We're going to sell it for a contract for deed," her mother says, surprising Miriam with this phrase from the eighties.

"We figured you'd want to drive up sometime while you're home."

"Don't you'all want to come with me?"

"The water's been turned off," her mother says. "It's so cold up there this time of year."

"We've run up and down that road enough to last a lifetime," her father says.

"You go on and go," her mother says, looking at Miriam.

Miriam borrows her mother's car to drive the forty miles to Table Rock. This is her favorite drive. She likes the kudzu-covered banks, the pine forests, the country barns, and the blue mountains rising before her. As soon as she is on this road, she gets a kind of peaceful blank feeling, like meditation. It seems that all of the roads of her life lead back to this one.

She drives through Marietta, the country town with the pretty name where her father was raised. It is hardly a place at all, just a crossroads with a filling station; the general store has been replaced by a 7–Eleven. The big white house where her father was born looks as if it ought to belong to some prominent personage in town, the town doctor perhaps. But her father's father was the town postman.

Directly behind the big house, about a "holler away," as her father might say, is the farmhouse of their country relatives, Loona and Cloys. They used to stop at their place on the way to the cabin. Loona and Cloys had a junk pile bigger than their house in their red-dirt yard. Wild cats peered from dark spaces there, but Miriam could never coax them up. They had an outhouse, and a mule which broke Miriam's heart with its mulish existence. She promised herself that when she grew up, she would buy him, and give him a life of leisure and pleasure.

Now as she drives slowly by on the highway, Miriam tries to see what has become of their place. Some years ago, her mother wrote her that Cloys had died of a heart attack, and more recently, that Loona was in a nursing home. Miriam wonders what became of the old mule. But, of course, he must have been dead for years now.

She drives out of Marietta, towards the mountains, slate blue on this winter day.

Then Table Rock Mountain comes into view. It seems near enough to touch; she could reach out her hand. She has climbed to the top many times. A trail leads up from behind the naturalist's office in the state park. It amazed her the first time she got to the top to see how round and small the lake looked from up there.

She turns up the little dirt road that leads to the cabin. Her summer days used to culminate in the early evening when she'd walk down this road to wait for her father to come home from work. She wanted to be the first to see him. She knew the sound of his station wagon far away. At last he would swing around the curve, turn up their dirt road, roll to a stop in a sputter of loose rock at the culvert, and Miriam would climb in beside him. His car always smelled of fresh roasted peanuts which he got at the filling station on the way up. There beside him was the evening paper, rolled and held with a rubber band.

The road is still dirt and loose rock. She has to go slow. When she rounds the bend, she sees the cabin. It is dark red with white trim. She sits in the car in the yard, looking at it.

A memory comes to her, of a summer day, when a bull from some neighboring farm wandered into the big open space meant for parking cars and turning around, where she now sits. The bull took turns chasing and being chased by their boxer dog Blaze, while Miriam and her sister Linda and their cousins Jimmy and Johnny whooped and hollered from the top of their mother's car.

Now everything is still and deserted. There is a profound stillness, and silence. Miriam gets slowly out of the car. She can almost feel superimposed on this winter scene the animation and noise of that summer day.

She walks over the flat stepping stones to the wooden steps. They had to have the steps replaced five or six years ago, when they finally rotted through. The padlock on the screen door opens easily with a key, and she hooks the lock, as they always have, back in the metal loop so it won't be lost. They must have been taught that as children. Her hands did it so automatically.

On the porch everything is just the same—the long pine table with its cold metal chairs that gave a chill when you sat down on them in shorts; the Pawley's Island hammock; the swinging sofa with green vinyl cushions.

She sees on closer inspection that a few things are gone.

But they have left the seashell ashtrays, and the card table is folded and propped against the inside wall, away from the screen, where rain might blow in.

She unlocks the big wooden door that opens into the living room. A gust of cold air sweeps past her, as if it were trapped inside and can now rush free. It is colder inside the cabin than outside. Miriam is glad. She won't be able to stay long.

Everything is just as it always is. The couches are covered in brown-and-white material, trimmed with a border print of hunting dogs and leaping fish. No one in her family has ever hunted or fished. The material must have looked like a "cabin" motif when her mother picked it out. There are two rockers, the ancient TV in the corner, an upright piano, the round hooked rug, and the fireplace made of fieldstones. Over the mantel are three wire ducks in various stages of taking off. They are staggered up the wall, higher and higher. These ducks have been taking off in just this formation for as long as Miriam can remember.

She goes in the back bedroom, her old room. There is the little Jenny Lind bed, and the big double bed; the three-drawer dresser; the sink that stands out from the wall. The high windows which open outwards. The curtains of red her mother made.

In her parents' room she sees that their dressing table is bare. They have removed the doily and her mother's pin tray and earring box, and her father's old black radio is gone from beside the bed. It is a four-poster bed. Miriam opens their dresser, which is empty now, and clean.

In the kitchen she opens the yellow cupboard. It is full of the tiger glasses they got one year at the Esso station, and the dishes with pine cones her mother collected at the Winn

Dixie. She sees an old enamel bowl in which she made tossed salads when they had the lifeguards from the state park over for spaghetti dinners, and the canning jars, empty now of her mother's blackberry jam.

She goes downstairs, to Linda's old room. Once a swarm of honey bees took up residence between the inside and outside walls, so that her room literally buzzed. Their father called a bee man, and from inside, Miriam and Linda watched him extract the queen, and take the bees away in a portable hive. He had been covered from head to toe in netting.

She goes back upstairs and stands in the cold living room. For a moment she imagines that they are all here. The cabin hums again with her parents, her sister, her aunts and uncles and cousins. Her aunt Alma, dead now of cancer, calls to her from the kitchen where she is cutting a bright crumbling ham, arranging pieces on a platter for Miriam to carry to the big table on the porch. Her mother is forking steaming ears of pale corn from an enormous boiler on the stove. Her father comes in from his garden, holding up Big Boy tomatoes for them to admire. Jimmy and Johnny are swinging too high in the hammock. The house reverberates with motion and noise and voices. For a moment the voices fill her head. Then everything evaporates into the silence of this winter day.

At the airport there is another goodbye. She hugs her mother; she embraces her father. There are tears all around, which everyone pretends don't exist.

Back in Minnesota, winter stretches out, long and cold. But Miriam doesn't mind. She spends her days writing, and what is writing after all but loyalty, the refusal to let go.

Spring comes, and her parents sell the cabin. A dentist and his wife buy it. They have three children under the age of ten.

When Miriam talks to her folks, she hears that they are relieved. "They're such nice people!" her mother says. And now the cabin will be used, enjoyed again.

Miriam notes that she doesn't feel too bad. When she tells Ted, she doesn't even cry. But when she tries to go near the cabin in her memory—she feels something akin to pain. She backs off. She thinks of something else.

Finally it is summer again in Minnesota. Almost overnight things turn lush and green. Their neighbor's yard, which has been totally exposed to view, is now obscured by a gigantic lilac bush. It is time to go to Rainbo again.

It is five o'clock on a Friday afternoon before they can leave the city, and it is after nine before they reach the North Woods. For the first time Miriam recognizes the point at which they are truly there—the fir trees smell a deeper, richer green. Now, every few miles as they speed along, the red eyes of deer shine from the side of the dark road, where they are grazing.

They do not stop for dinner until they reach Minocqua. They are heading for a supper club they've stopped at before. The place has Christmas lights strung around the bar, stuffed fish and mounted deer heads on the walls, and a menu specializing in prime rib and walleye pike. Out the window is a little scene in which plaster deer reminiscent of Bambi are spotlighted beside an artificial waterfall.

Ted takes Miriam's hand and holds it. They are getting a little drunk on gin and tonics while they wait for their dinner.

"Do you realize we might never have met?" Ted says. "What if one of us hadn't signed up for that creative writing class? What if there were two sections and I went on Monday nights and you went on Wednesdays?"

Miriam laughs, but actually she has thought of this before. After all it is so random really, accidental after all, the way two people meet. And what if they had never met? This thought is so stunning to Miriam, so unthinkable really, that she clutches Ted's hand with both of hers, and holds on for dear life.

It is well after midnight when they pull into the grass yard at Rainbo. They get the key from the hiding place, and let themselves in. Ted immediately looks for his fishing cap. It isn't his, really—maybe it was his grandfather's—but it always hangs on a peg in the hall, along with all the slickers and other gear. All the relatives who use Rainbo are always careful to put things back, but Ted's fishing cap—the one he always wears at Rainbo—is missing. Ted can't believe it. "It's got to be here," he says, tearing from room to room, looking in all the closets and drawers. "I can't go fishing without that cap," he says, only half joking. "I bet one of my cousins stole it!"

He goes in the living room and picks up the little book that everyone writes in after their weekends at Rainbo. People tend to wax poetic in their entries, showing off with warm feelings—"wonderful friends, wonderful food, wonderful weather"—that sort of thing. Ted pretends to write in the little book, "Where's my goddamn hat? Ted." Miriam laughs out loud.

When he settles down, they sit in the kitchen under the yellow light, eating Fig Newtons and drinking milk someone has left in the refrigerator. They take showers in the fragrant cedar-lined shower. And when Miriam comes into the bedroom, Ted is in bed in his blue pajamas, and he looks, well,—so beautiful—to Miriam. His hair is tousled and wet, and she rests her eyes on his wonderful, handsome face—all that personality, that animation.

She takes off her robe and gets in bed. She presses the side of her face against his, and feels his warm skin. He entwines his legs with hers.

They've talked, theoretically, over the past year about having a child. Miriam has never been sure. She's never felt certain. But just now, when she came into the bedroom, she caught a glimpse of the future: three of them, out in a boat on a summer day at Rainbo.

In the morning when she wakes it is raining very softly. Ted sleeps beside her, beautiful still. The rain on the roof sounds exactly the way the rain on the roof used to sound at the cabin. And then it all comes back to her, how she used to lie in the Jenny Lind bed, surrounded by golden walls, listening to the sound of rain.

When the rain lets up in the afternoon, they go out in the boat. Miriam brings her journal along, but mainly she spends her time rowing them over to shore, where Ted is constantly getting his line caught on some log or limb. He has caught several small fish, which he calls teen burgers. Miriam tries to describe in her journal the light on the water, and the fir trees around the lake. She sees in the deep serious green a bright glow underneath, like an internal combustion.

Ted is wearing his red flannel shirt and the old fishing cap, which Miriam found under some jackets this morning. He keeps up a running monologue of self-deprecating jokes about his fishing, and Miriam sees that he is happy.

Some ducks fly overhead, quacking as they go, circling the lake, and then landing. Miriam sees their orange legs, and the way they skid onto the water. She starts to write a description of them, but something startles, or beckons them, and they take off, their orange legs running along the water, and then they rise, one, two, three, higher and higher, the familiar formation, shouting as they go.

Miriam looks down at her paper. Writing is her way to not let go. To keep them all alive. For if she writes clearly and simply enough about her father—how he wipes his shoes off on the back of his pants legs before he goes out the door—and if she describes accurately the smokey blue of her mother's eyes as she tells her daughter goodbye at the airport—and if she captures on paper the sound of Ted's lovely, funny voice—*then won't they live forever? Won't they never die?*

"I've got one!" Ted exclaims. "Or maybe it's only a log."

Ted's rod is actually bending. And there it is, a big fish, rising to the surface. Ted calls for the net, but Miriam catches it on the tackle box, and Ted has to take time to undo it. Finally it is in the boat, a sluggish northern with saw teeth. Naturally it has taken the hook deep. Ted and Miriam look at each other and grimace, but Ted gets to work with the long-nosed pliers. He uses them to hold the northern's mouth open. It would prefer to keep it shut, Miriam thinks. She sits on the boat seat with her hands between her knees. Ted does his best. There is a puddle of blood on the yellow boat cushion.

"These things are practically indestructible," Ted says.

He holds the northern in the water by the side of the boat so Miriam can see that it is all right. Blood and tissue float away. It gives a wiggle and is gone.

"They have great healative powers," Miriam says. She doesn't know if "healative" is a word.

"Catching a northern feels a lot like catching a log," Ted says.

A little later, he says "uh oh," and points. They see a big fish out on the surface, floating on its side, arched so its head and tail rise for a long moment out of the water. Then it disappears.

"That couldn't be it," Ted says hopefully. "We're too far from where we put it back."

"That's it," Miriam says. "I recognized its face."

They motor to another part of the lake.

"Maybe I'll have better luck here," Ted says. "Maybe I won't catch one."

"I know where you can catch a big one with a shovel," Miriam says and laughs.

Later they see a black-and-white eagle sweep over the lake. It dives down to the water, and flies away with something large in its claws.

"Now you don't have to feel so bad," Ted says. "We're feeding the eagles."

Miriam smiles to herself. She watches the eagle disappear over the trees.

About the Author

Paulette Bates Alden was born and raised in Greenville, South Carolina. She received her M.A. in writing from Stanford University, where she was a Stegner Fellow. She has taught at Stanford and is currently Writer in Residence at the University of Minnesota, where she is a member of the adjunct faculty.

Colophon

Feeding the Eagles
was designed by Scott Walker.
The Sabon type was set by
Typeworks (Vancouver, B.C.).
The book was manufactured by
Edwards Brothers (Ann Arbor).

Library of Congress Cataloging-in-Publication Data

Alden, Paulette Bates, 1947-
　　Feeding the eagles : short stories / by Paulette Bates Alden.
　　　　p.　cm. -- (The Graywolf short fiction series)
　　　ISBN 1-55597-111-3 : $16.00
　　　I. Title.　II. Series.

PS3551.L334F44 1988
　813'.54--dc 19　　　　　　　　　　　　　　　　　88-15621
　　　　　　　　　　　　　　　　　　　　　　　　　　CIP